DEADLY ALLY

Deadly Ally

*Mountain Warriors
Book 2*

R.J. BURLE

Pier House Books

To my parents, Ray and Jean, who inspired me to be what I am today. My father taught me tenacity to chase my goals with fierce determination. My mother gave me the wisdom to know that changing tactics or setting my sites on better goals is not quitting.

PROLOGUE

The terror confined itself like a peach pit deep in his belly. He kept his eyes open, scanning the dark trail in front of him. Under black leather gloves, his hands white knuckled the plastic grips of his M-16. Douglas Bircher had faced terror before. He had served an enlistment in the Army's infantry and visited deadly hot spots in the War on Terror-- a terror that in no way matched what currently gnawed at his gut.

Douglas now served in Craigsville's (or the Lowboys as the Mountain Warriors called them) security police where he had seen even more horror at home after the recent scourge of zombism, but surrounded by capable fighters he always felt like he had a fighting chance. Now he felt like he was being led like livestock to the slaughter. The loaded M-16 felt like a useless weight in his hands because worse than the zombies, the vampires horrified Douglas.

Douglas and three of his companions, all hardened fighters, currently marched under The Specter's command. They had set off at sunset, and The Specter led them past the point where they usually dropped off condemned prisoners. No one had ever gone past there, until now, and they headed straight into the heart of the vampires' killing ground.

There were dark whispered rumors of the prisoners who were condemned to death getting devoured by vampires, but in these days one never knew the difference between rumor versus fact versus folklore versus propaganda versus the news. However, marching through the vampires' killing grounds brought the horror from whispered lore into stark reality as Douglas and the other men walked through where no human was known to have survived.

The moon lit up the pale disintegrating faces of those dead human remains drained of blood by the vampires. The bodies lay on the ground or were propped against trees and boulders where they had been dumped. Long after suffering their fates, their mouths were still open in permanent death screams of abysmal pain. Between the winter's cold and the appearance of having all vital nutrients drained, the hollow remains of the human victims did not decay as quickly. Scavengers like raccoons, opossums, bacteria, and even the zombies, who were mindless eaters, avoided these dead.

After leaving the killing field far behind, Douglas and his compatriots went consistently upward on the trail. Sweat poured from Douglas's skin against the cold night.

The Specter was a tall, broad, and strong man-like figure in black paramilitary fatigues, hooded cloak that flowed darkly with the brisk march, and a terrifyingly realistic skull faced mask. He was armed with a submachine gun strapped to his shoulder, a handgun at his waist, as well as a sword, and probably an array of concealed weaponry.

The Specter said not a word after he gave the initial order, "Follow me," and no one dared to ask anything further. That was eight hours and many miles of marching ago. It was now well past midnight, yet dawn was still far away.

Douglas thought he hallucinated when on the side of the trail, he saw a large block of ice reflecting the sickly moonlight. He removed a black leather glove to touch the car sized chunk only to realize that it was quartz. He guessed that they were in the Shining Rock Wilderness area and nearing the summit. He had heard rumors that the vampires occupied a mythical labyrinth of passages beneath the white rock mountain top. From local Cherokee legend, the tunnels were believed to be a mix of natural caverns and passages carved by the inhuman hands of the *Nunnehi.* Douglas looked up and saw that they were about a half mile beneath Shining Rock's peak. It rose above them like a snow covered head and shoulder of a sleeping giant.

They marched past hordes of zombies whose eyes lit up with unnatural hunger and unliving but animated muscles bunched ready to pounce upon the living. However, their eyes quickly glazed over and their muscles fell slack with a mere glance from The Specter. The soldiers had never walked this close to zombies without engaging in mortal combat, yet somehow The Specter's unnatural power over the undead gave the soldiers no relief from their deep terrors. It had the opposite effect to the point that Douglas feared his temporary leader more than he feared the zombies.

The four men watched curiously as The Specter walked straight toward a quartzite cliff near the summit as if he planned to walk through the impenetrable crystal. The soldiers stopped and stared in disbelief. Walking through was exactly what he did. It seemed as if the rock wobbled and melted like a waterfall, allowing the giant, whose humanity was already in doubt, to pass through the shimmering rock like a ghost.

From the other side of the rock the voice of The Specter boomed "Why did you stop? Move." The sound of his voice assaulted their ears as if no solid object separated them. Yet he had disappeared behind the rock face.

The four soldiers followed hesitantly and stepped through the rock as if it wasn't there. With the realization that the rockface blocking the entrance was an illusion, Douglas scoped the inside of the cave, not knowing what to expect, eyes wide, on full alert, attempting to see in the cavernous gloom. After walking through the rock, he suspiciously studied everything.

The Specter turned back to the crystal passage and growled in a voice that seemed to mock a charming, cheery voice of a tour guide, "Welcome to the Cavern of the Vampire's Castle. These tunnels lay empty until the laboratories that produced the vampiric virus just a few years ago reinvigorated them with their experimentation in psionic abilities." The sarcasm felt like a knife to Douglas after the hours of reticence from their imposing leader.

Douglas looked above at the quartzite dome that let defuse moon and starlight trickle inside, giving a somewhat surreal and heavenly ambience. Despite his fear, Douglas mentioned his awe.

The Specter replied back, "That is if you feel at home and in heaven with vampires and other monstrosities of advanced scientific witchery," he finished with a cruel rumbling laugh.

The Specter called forth into the passage in his unnaturally deep voice, "Richard, I have arrived."

"We all welcome you, Specter," An aristocratic and slightly nasal toned voice echoed from the yawning black maw of the cavern.

The four men strained their eyes in the weak light to see who The Specter addressed. As their eyes adjusted, they saw a man in a black hooded cloak who was already tall and slender, but seemed towering with arrogance despite being unsettled by the presence of The Specter. As the soldiers drew nearer behind their skull-faced leader and saw the figures behind Richard, fifteen in all, their eyes widened in disbelief. The terror that Douglas and his companions had formerly kept hidden, now lit their eyes.

"I did not tell you to stop," The Specter growled over his shoulder at the four soldiers.

The four men stepped forward and confirmed their suspicion. They looked at the black cloaks, the hoods that lay across the shoulders, the pale skin, and the hunger in the beings' eyes as they looked the soldiers over like they were livestock.

The cave dwellers were all vampires. About fifteen in all. However only six had the steadiness of human sanity and intelligence in their eyes that were bright with barely controlled bloodlust.

On the other hand, the other vampires seemed over-whelmed by the thirst for human blood. These appeared no better than the savage zombies outside, with dull emotionless faces, flashing fangs and ravenous eyes. Their exposed skin was crisscrossed with lacerations. Douglas guessed that their desire to feed their bloodlust overrode their instincts to pro-tect themselves from the last ditch human defense of finger-nails and teeth.

Douglas also noticed that the six intelligent looking vamps were armed with rifles and handguns as well as swords. He saw that the lesser intelligent ones carried no guns but had swords and clubs, while the stupidest and most savage carried no weapons at all. However, the uncontrolled, crazed look in their eyes worried him more than the ones with weapons.

One of the more primal vampires emitted a low growl that grew steadily into an ear piercing shriek. Douglas flinched as he watched the vamp, overcome with the lust, charge at them. The Specter backhanded the creature and sent him flying backwards fifteen feet into the cave's wall.

"Stand down! You will feed, only when I allow!" The Specter savagely barked in a military commanding voice.

The cavernous hall was silent for a moment after the echo of his order died. The scolded vampire whimpered and slouched in the back of the formation with his fellow vamps.

A beautiful young vampiress looked at the soldiers. She was one of the six intelligent ones. She didn't have the same hunger blazing in her deep soulful eyes, but rather an expressive concern for the fate of the men. Douglas could almost hear a command from her screaming in his mind, "run," although her lips did not move.

He exchanged looks with his fellow soldiers. Their eyes told each other that something controlled their minds. They had heard that the vampires had psionic powers of hypnosis and telepathy, but very few people survived to tell of an encounter with them.

However, neither Douglas nor his comrades could move. Something had firm control over their wills. Their feet seemed to have solidified into the stone bedrock floor of the cavern. Over the woman's mental voice, something else seemed to have taken control over their bodies and minds, even more powerful than The Specter's commands. Their terror mounted as they took in all the sights and conflicting psychic commands. Their minds almost crushed with mental overload, they could only stand and watch as The Specter scolded them.

"Give me your weapons. You are insulting our hosts." He rumbled as he grabbed their M-16s and tossed them with a clatter like refuse into an aperture of the cave . The Specter however kept his armament on his person.

A large vampire, named David, who was built like a linebacker on a professional football team and had a face like a punching bag, walked up and without patting them down, took their hidden knives and handguns as if he read their minds as to where they concealed such objects.

Richard cleared his throat and said, "Specter, we need to talk about The Mind. He consumes so much that we are over harvesting people for blood. The local villages know it is us. If humanity unites against us..."

"I have brought food for you and him," The Specter rumbled.

"Four?" Richard said with a slight whine.

Terror inspired adrenalin pounded through the soldier's veins, but they were so frozen, rooted into the ground that they could not even look at each other from the corner of their eyes.

The Specter replied, "These specimens are strong. Vital warrior blood floods their veins. Any one of them is worth the blood of three regular men."

"We need more," Richard complained as he and his brood eyed the soldiers like a starving wolf pack would stare at a flock of lambs.

"You get the blood. The Mind will get the drained bodies," The Specter announced dismissively.

"Run," the young vampiress kept saying without speaking aloud.

Douglas made eye contact with her and immediately knew that the vampiress' name was Abigail. He could not fathom how he acquired that knowledge. He just knew.

She kept psychically telling him to leave, but he stood frozen, helpless as if in a dream. Something else had control. Douglas instinctively knew that whatever The Mind was, it had full control over him.

"Let me see him. The Mind," The Specter demanded.

"Yes, my lord," said Richard.

The vampires turned and walked further into the crystal mountain. The vampiress gave the soldiers one last look of warning and then walked with her kind. The Specter followed. Although the soldiers didn't know what The Mind was, the psychic power pulled them to their doom. That pull was more powerful than their will to survive, and despite the terror that the soldiers felt about going deeper into the seeming abyss of the abhorrent caverns, none of the vampires had to prod them.

The deeper they went, the darker the gloom seemed to settle around their bodies and spirits, so much so that they were resigned to whatever fate awaited them. Douglas actually felt relaxed through most of his body.

"The Mind takes up so much energy," said Richard.

"If he was purely machine, he would need a hundred times more gallons of fossil fuel than blood." The Specter then said as if repeating an advertising jingle, "Blood; an ecologically sound and renewable fuel source for a sustainable future. Don't you vampires like feeling green?" The Specter rumbled something that resembled a laugh at his own poor joke. Otherwise the underground hall was silent but for their footfalls.

They arrived at a balcony carved from the crystal that overlooked a huge cathedral-like room. The room was the brightest point of the caves. The top of the ceiling was pure quartz and let in much star and moonlight. So much that the more intelligent vampires instinctively put up their hoods out of habit of shielding themselves from too much light. Another source of lights came from the rows of computer banks that lined the walls that ringed the balconies.

At the bottom, some thirty feet below them was something that resembled a huge man, almost twenty feet tall, so large that he couldn't escape into human sized tunnels that connected to his cathedral sized room. He could hardly hold up his overly enlarged head that was about the size of his naked chest and abdomen. Wires attached to his skull wove a maze around him. His immensely muscular arms dragged the cavern's floor. In the dim light the soldiers couldn't see any other features, but they had a sense of immense deformity.

The soldiers stood where The Specter had ordered them to stop as he peered down at the gigantic man monster who hungrily stared back up at them.

"He is brilliant," rumbled The Specter.

"Maybe, but he is insane while awake," Richard whispered.

The Mind roared at them, "I can not think clearly without fuel."

"That is why we're here, my friend." The Specter shouted to The Mind. Then he turned to Richard, "Can you blame him? He can hook into the knowledge of life and computers. He truly knows all. He's only insane when awake because he's hungry."

Indeed The Mind was a marvel. His cyborg, biocomputer mind tapped into computers and acted as an antennae for the psionic power utilized by the vampires. Although horrendously ugly to look at and ill tempered when awake, the ability to have developed a brain that could both tap into the internet as well as the neural impulses of other sentient beings was a marvel of modern research. Although The Mind was considered to be a crude prototype of what could be eventually achieved. The Specter gazed in awe at the monstrosity and said, "He is beautiful, but hungry."

"We are hungry too, my lord," said Richard, disturbing The Specter's admiration of the abomination below the balcony.

Indeed it had been torture for the vampires to walk with the soldiers without making a move to feed their desires. The vampires of lesser intelligence only held back because of their fear of The Specter, but Douglas could sense that resolve was weakening as they whimpered, growled and gnashed their fangs.

"I am working on getting regular blood for you," replied The Specter. "We will call for talks with the humans and make a deal for providing our protection for the people against the zombies. In return they will voluntarily gift their blood to you."

"I hope it works," said Richard. The lead vampire shifted with a deep seated agitation.

"What is it, Richard?" The Specter asked, knowing full well the torture that the vampire suffered.

"May we?" Richard asked.

The rest of the vamps hungrily asked the question with their eyes as they moved back and forth on their feet. The more insane ones growled and whined as they crowded forward toward the disarmed soldiers. The soldiers stood still, powerless against the mind control.

"Of course my friends," said The Specter with his rumbling laugh.

Richard approached the nearest soldier. A slim dagger appeared in his long thin hand as Richard casually raised it from his belt beneath the cloak.

"Relax," Richard purred in a soothing voice. Despite the threat of the double edged knife approaching his throat, the soldier visibly obeyed and relaxed although his eyes were widened with horror.

The other soldiers stared in wide eyed trepidation, locked into place by an unspoken command. The voice from the pretty vampiress also screamed in the deepest recesses of their minds, "Run," but they could not obey her nor their deepest instincts. "Ignore the pull and take control of your body and soul," her mental voice shouted, but Douglas found that to be impossible.

They watched as Richard quickly and expertly penetrated the dagger into the throat of the soldier with the skill of a surgeon. The knife was seen as more civilized than a savage bite, and there was no chance of accidentally turning a victim into a vampire who might in turn seek revenge if his mind wasn't ravaged by the change.

The soldier screamed once and stopped as Richard lovingly stroked his chest. The other soldiers watched rigidly with their peripheral vision, knowing that they were next, but helpless to do anything.

The dagger directly pierced the carotid artery, rewarding Richard with a spurting wound of blood which David adroitly collected in a bowl shaped like an extra large golden goblet after Richard removed the dagger, and took the goblet from David to collect the rest of the blood. The other vampires hovered around as if ready to pounce as David the largest, strongest vampire held the soldier up so he wouldn't collapse as he was drained of his life blood.

When the soldier was about to succumb, The Specter grabbed him by the scruff of the neck and tossed him off of the balcony into the large room below. The brutal impact reverberated seconds later. The twenty foot tall giant lumbered to the shattered body and soon the sounds of crunching bones and smacking lips echoed through the chamber.

Through the haze of the mind control that froze his body, Douglas was confused as to whether The Mind was something of their leader or a prisoner. Douglas sensed that the twenty foot tall creature below him caused him to freeze in place, but The Mind oddly seemed to be at the mercy of The Specter and the vampires.

"He still had more blood," protested David. It was known that the big vampire took an almost sensual pleasure to suck any remaining blood from the victim's body as it still weakly writhed in protest before fading into death. David also enjoyed snapping the neck to ensure they wouldn't return to unnatural life.

Richard took a few hungry sips from the gallon sized goblet. He sighed in pleasure and passed the goblet to David. Richard wanted more.

"The Mind needed to eat," The Specter replied.

"So do we," Richard said back with respect but also a hint of desperation.

"Do not forget your purpose, vampire," The Specter scolded. "The Mind, by himself, fulfils the psionic experiments more than all of you vampires combined."

In this moment, with everyone's guard down as the vampires focused on the goblet of blood and The Mind viciously and noisily crunched on the bones, the young vampiress quickly turned her gaze to the three remaining soldiers and shot the thought, "Run," into their heads. As The Mind crunched on the bones, his power waned from the distraction. "Run!" Abigail instructed again.

She looked directly into Douglas's eyes. For a moment her essence took up his entire perception. "Run!" her command shot through his head and then flashed through his body like an electric bolt. That sparked an explosive reaction inside of him and the three remaining soldiers. With The Mind's focus on the body, Abigail grabbed the reins of whatever controlled them. The soldiers took off and raced back to the entrance.

"Get them," barked The Specter.

The young vampiress obeyed the order and sprinted after them, the first to give chase, but The Specter grabbed her by the long locks of her dark hair. He yanked her off of her feet by his restraint and her momentum. The other vampires except David and Richard raced past her.

"Not you, Abigail," The Specter roared.

She angrily flashed her fangs at him, her face contorted monstrously with her rage and defiance. He slapped her across her face. Her continence became passive as he wrapped his enormous hand around her graceful throat, but her eyes ever defiant, looked up into his.

"How did they break the spell of The Mind, vampiress?" he demanded.

"I do not know, master. He must have been distracted by his meal." she answered. Her eyes softened, innocent deep wells to her soul.

The Specter took the goblet from David and handed it to her. The Specter watched her closely, looking for any sign of human compassion.

"Drink," he commanded.

She glared back at him as she took the blood filled goblet. Defiance again flashed in her eyes as she looked pointedly at The Specter as she drank. She drank deeply, hungrily.

Richard angrily yanked at the goblet, but not before she had taken more than her fair share, still trying to drink even as David pulled her away. The whole time her eyes never left The Specter's.

The Specter grunted and then ordered her to join the chase. "Go!" His finger seemed to violently strike the air as he pointed in the direction.

She glared at him one last time and ran off.

"I don't like her," The Specter growled at Richard when she was out of earshot. "How trustworthy is she?"

"She isn't," David instead replied.

Richard glared at David before he answered The Specter, "Of all of us, she has the most powerful psionic abilities, by far. Even I don't understand what she has. She had the powers long before we turned her. When my mind first connected with hers before she turned, it unlocked something in her psyche. We really do not know her full potential. It's very similar to that journalist, Eric Hildebrande, who you just released into our domain."

"I did not ask of her abilities. I asked of her trustworthiness. She can cut off the hive mind. How do you know you can trust her?" The Specter pressed.

Richard cast David a stern, threatening look before he replied. David glared back under hooded eyelids.

"I turned her myself," Richard said. "I am her father by the vampiric bloodline."

"But you pursued her for a year. Every successful vampire willingly conforms to the transformation, if they want immortality. She resisted violently, yet didn't become one of these idiotic failed vampires."

"Nine months we chased her, but she finally agreed to become one of us," Richard protested.

"For nine months she fled and fought you. That sounds more like a disagreement than an agreement," said The Specter. "How many vampires did she kill before she was turned?"

"She is one of us," Richard stated firmly ignoring his last question. "Very few of us keep our sanity. If she was turned against her will she would have been one of the failed or worse. Most of the vampires are little better than zombies if at all, you know that. I, myself, have to fight every day not to turn into, into…" Richard couldn't finish his thought, but finished with, "She could almost pass for human with her self control."

"That's what worries me," The Specter replied. "Is it control or does she favor humans over her own kind? But no worries, the blood work of the journalist who you almost killed last night, Eric Hildebrande, shows great potential for replacing her."

Richard stepped forward and firmly proclaimed, "She is one of us. She is loyal. I am staking my immortal life on her."

The Mind looked up from his meal as The Specter's mocking laughter echoed through the vampire's caverns.

"Yes, you are," The Specter agreed.

David quietly looked into the direction that Abigail had disappeared.

Continued reports from Eric Hildebrande's investigations in the Forbidden Zone:

| 1 |

In a dark cocoon, something restrained my arms and legs.
I heard an erratic ticking like my heart and mind were wired
as if I was a living time bomb.

Tick. Tock. Pause. Tick tick tick tock pause.

The pauses held me in suspense, but dreamy paralysis
gripped me.

Tick. Tock tock tick tick. Splat.

The ticking became wet.   Something dripped on my tent.
I struggled and felt that the restraint was just my sleeping
bag. I was vaguely aware that I was half asleep. My mind was
shot through with visions of the battle from last night. In my
dreams, I relived the advance of the thousands of undead and
saw them fall beneath the lightning swords of me and my new
tribe as we held the line. But it wasn't a dream. It actually occurred just hours before. I realized this as my mind sank back
into the black dreamscape. I dreamt of slain zombies hanging like macabre ornaments from the trees above, dripping

their infectious ochre on my tent as their dead eyes stared into space.

My eyes instantly blinked open, my mind wide awoke as I shot to a sitting position. I reached for my sword. The hilt felt comfortable in my grip. It was a short sword, called a wakizashi in Japanese. It looked like a katana's kid brother. The wak was about two feet long instead of three. The smaller length almost got me killed last night when I faced the vampires. I vowed to get a hold of a more formidable weapon today.

After feeling the relief of the sword in my hand, I looked to the gaps in the tent. I expected to see the red light of dawn slipping inside like the reaching edges of a pool of spilled blood, but it was still night. I guessed it was nearing dawn from the light stirrings of the camp.

I listened further and realized the drops falling like drum beats on my thread bare tarp tent were simply fresh water from the heavy nightly dew, not blood and ochre. From the cold in the tent, I was surprised that the dew was not frozen into frost.

Just two days ago, I had sat in comfort outside the quarantine zone. I had asked for this assignment into the Forbidden Zone, and my friend, Tommy, obliged. Now life behind the fences was less about filming a documentary and more about staying alive. Now I relied on a band of survivors to protect me even though they didn't fully trust me, and for good reason. I had lied to them by omission rather than open dishonesty. In my defense, I didn't fully understand what was going on.

I was the one who had triggered the zombie attack last night when I accidentally discharged a handgun during training. Later, I was credited with being the first person to slay one of the vampires, Abigail, when she was merely unconscious at my feet.

Outside the tent, I heard a few men discussing the plans for today in deep steady voices. I couldn't hear the exact words, just the low serious tones. I recognized Bryan's voice, he was the second in command of this camp of about fifty or so survivors and head war chief in times of panic.

So many people continually came and went that I could never get a full count. Even if I could get a count, I didn't want to get caught counting the members. Although I felt like I was accepted into the tribe after last night's battle, paranoia gnawed at my gut. Deep inside I was certain that some here still thought I was a spy. If someone thought they could confirm that suspicion even on the weakest evidence, I had no doubt that I would be instantly executed.

I didn't recognize the other voices outside my tent. Critter, the trapper and woodsman among woodsmen, was probably in the conversation, but he rarely spoke and usually it was to issue sharp commands or grunts of agreement or dissent.

Since I couldn't hear the words of the conversation, my mind drifted back to that woman, the vampiress who occupied my thoughts. A woman who may not even be human. Abigail. Did she want me to live, or did she want me dead or undead? I had only glimpsed her briefly in person and exchanged a handful of spoken words. I felt like I knew her all my life, yet she felt like my greatest enigma, and I had no idea why, other than she seemed to actually visit me in my dreams.

Needing to face the day, I unzipped the sleeping bag and firmly pushed away its warm cover, as well at the wool blanket I had over me. I grudgingly stood, slightly bent over, under the low hanging tarp roof. My hair was instantly damp when it touched the dew drenched roof. I tried to ignore the biting cold in the tent. I didn't want to get caught sleeping in late for fear of getting made fun of like the day before.

I had slept in my clothes from the night before. They were clean and warm when I put them on after the battle. It was wise to sleep fully clothed, because the warrior lifestyle could see you awakened to a literal fight for your life at any moment, and you did not want to get caught outside in a battle, undressed in freezing weather.

I grabbed my recording equipment to continue my documentary on life in the Forbidden Zone, slid the sword in its scabbard into my belt, and stepped out of the tent. I forced myself to stand straight against muscles sore from combat. I had to present myself as formidable to my new tribe where any suggestion of weakness was scorned. I soon forgot about my appearance as I took in the sights around the camp. It was a visual assault on my soul.

A few fires lit the camp at zero dark thirty, and I could see the dark shapes of survivors moving about their business. Just beyond the circle of tarp hovels, bodies of the undead lay everywhere twisted together in a profane embrace of bloody pale grey arms, legs, and torsos. Enough were cleared from the immediate center of camp to let the younger children play somewhat safely near the communal fire, but, "My God," I half swore and half prayed.

Most bodies were still. I could see one zombie who's torso was cut off beneath the neck, leaving one arm reaching and the jaws snapping for anything to devour. Hundreds of entangled limbs still moved in unnatural spasms en masse giving a feeling of a mirage. Occasionally a monstrous groan or scream from one of them wracked my body. There was just enough human pain in the cries to touch both my compassion and terror.

I instinctively looked up to the hills above for any potential enemies, human or undead. Nothing but the bare hibernating vegetation and stony landscape of the Appalachian Mountains met my eyes under the poor light of a sliver of the moon. Two drones buzzed around filming us. I wondered if Tommy or anyone that I knew was watching me at present. Footage from the quarantined area was top entertainment in the Safe Zones.

I stopped by Shelley's tarp teepee as I could see a glow of a small fire and saw the silhouette of her movements projected on the canvas wall. She was the camp's medicine woman. I knocked on the tarp and asked, "How's Peter?"

"Come in," she said in a sweet grandmotherly voice that disguised a spirit strong as steel. I opened the flap and ducked in and regretted it. Peter had fractured his leg just beneath his knee in the battle last night. I had seen the fibula bone poking through his skin. Now it was set and wrapped in bloody bandages, but his pain ravaged face touched my soul. Tylenol and whiskey were the only pain killers in the camp.

"Other than dying, I guess I am OK," Peter said with a forced laugh. He instantly grimaced as the laughter shook his body causing agony from his shattered wound.

"Anything that I can do?" I asked.

"Wave a magic wand over my broken leg?" Peter asked.

I pretended to wave a wand. It didn't help, but a smile did break his grimace.

Shelley said, "You and Bryan are going into one of the towns to get Peter some antibiotics."

"No rush," Peter said, still trying to appear immune to his own suffering.

"Baloney." Shelley said firmly. "Peter needs antibiotics and hopefully some decent pain killers within twenty four hours."

As my eyes adjusted to the dismally lighted tent, I could see it wasn't just blood but yellow pus that stained the bandages. I caught a faint scent of it and almost heaved. It was odd. The smell of the dead zombies was atrocious, but the milder smell of Peter's wound stirred me more. I knew that there was suffering behind that stench.

I quickly excused myself, "I'll go find Bryan, then."

They bade me goodbye. As I stepped out of the tent, I heard the greeting, "Good morning, Eric."

"Good morning, Bryan," I tried to sound respectful to the second in command of the tribe. Second in command was a loose term in this herd of cats. The camp was really run by a set of rules and protocols that everyone agreed with and were punished brutally over when broken. No one was above the set rules.

Bryan carried a sword and a handgun at his waist and a rifle of the AR-15 variation strapped to his back this morning. Firearms were ubiquitous but tended to be used only as a last resort due to the scarcity of bullets, but more importantly, a gunshot attracted the zombie hordes. My accidental discharge yesterday resulted in the battle last night.

"Where is your sword?" he asked.

"Here," I replied as I patted the hilt. "Why? Are we expecting an attack?" I asked.

"That's a stupid question. We always are. It's your job as a man to carry a sword at all times."

"Isn't that a bit patriarchal?" I joked.

Bryan didn't have a sense of humor this morning nor did he care for the PC climate of more civilized times, unless of course his wife was around to cast the eye upon him. His moods were as prone to change as the southern Appalachian weather. Today, he was stormy.

"What the hell are you talking about?" he shot at me.

"I was joking."

He smiled and said, "I know. Go get breakfast."

"You got it," I said and turned to go to the fire.

There were many honorable qualities about Bryan that I admired. However, I disliked his enjoyment at making me squirm. As well as getting a more formidable sword today, I was determined to do something about his mistreatment of me.

The sun started to break the horizon, and I couldn't help but wonder about Abigail. Was she hiding from the sun in some deep dank dungeon, cave or tomb with her loathsome kind?

***

Douglas Bircher swept through the dark woods on his run to escape from the Caverns of the Vampires. The black shadows of the hooded vamps flitted all around him in the chase. His blood pounded in his ears like the war drums of a pursuing tribe. His chest felt like it would implode as he couldn't take in any more air to fill his need for oxygen, but he would rather die of exhaustion than to face those things again. He had no idea how long he had run from that terrible cave of crystal, but at this point, it was purely base instinct that propelled him, driven by the howling bloodlust of those things.

Collapsing of exhaustion probably wasn't too far away. He would stumble as fast as he could for about twenty-five to fifty yards on clumsy, numbed feet that barely obeyed his brain and then would sprawl on his face from a root, or rock in his path. Obstacles were almost impossible to avoid in the nighttime woods anyway, but in his present state, the trip hazards seemed to seek him out. Sometimes an obstacle wasn't needed. It was pure fatigue that sprawled him on several occasions.

He not only wanted to save himself; he had to warn others back in his village. With those two desires, he pressed on.

During his run in the sheer panic through the dark forest, he had quickly lost contact with the other two surviving soldiers. After exiting through the quartz doorway they blindly plunged downhill. They couldn't see each other in the night and could barely see the many tree branches with which they often collided.

Once his initial panic calmed, and he realized he lost his comrades, he had rested where he had fallen over a root, but almost immediately he had heard the screams of one of his fellows far in the distance and howls of triumph of those vampire things crazed by their bloody capture. It was a scream he never expected a hardened soldier to ever make. It started out as a high pitched shrill of terror and lowered to a groan so deep as to emit from the most profound pit of hell as the man was drained and devoured. The terror voiced in that man's final moments had driven Douglas onward again. He would rather run to death, only hearing the crunch of the leaves beneath his combat boots than hear the screams of a comrade murdered again.

On one of his final sprawls, he lay in a panting heap, thinking it was finally safe to rest, or maybe it wasn't safe, but his body just refused to move. However, he forced himself to hold his labored breath so he could hear the surrounding forest.

What he heard sent him into a headlong panicked run again. The sound of a predator's feet crunching leaves, whispered above his thundering pulse and heavy gasping breaths. The footfalls were slightly muffled like that of a great cat that could stalk at a full run. He bounded to his feet with new energy and launched through the woods.

He felt a sense of hope as a red line was breaking on the mountainous eastern horizon. He wasn't sure if it was truth or lore about vampires' lives being confined to the night, but he had faith that the light of the sun would be his savior. It was a bit of a metaphor from his days in Sunday school as a kid. He fell again, stood up, started sprinting, and then after a time slowed to a light sustainable jog.

He kept catching the glimpse of a blackened shape, a figure of a person in the vampiric hooded cloak, who either trailed him, or came up on the side of Douglas as if corralling him in a certain direction. Whoever it was kept their distance, just enough to keep him moving but not close enough to catch him. He felt as if a great tiger was playing with him, savoring a playful hunt before the meal.

He pushed on and caught his foot on a root, twisted his ankle and sprawled one last time. He looked up in terror as he lay at the feet of a black cloaked, hooded thing. The figure in black raised a finger to its face where its lips would be. He could not see the face, only the blackened maw of the hood, but he recognized the universal signal for silence. He still thought it best to scream, but he found himself compelled to obey.

The figure moved its hood back as if to ready its mouth to eat as it squatted and leaned into him. He was about to scream, but he saw the face.

It was Abigail, the vampiress, who had warned him to run. The one who broke the spell and allowed the escape. He wondered if she was just a sadist who preferred a chase before killing. Maybe she wanted his blood only for herself. He could still see the hunger of bloodlust in her eyes, but he could see something else that may have been compassion. He wasn't sure which drive was in command of her at this moment.

"I think you are safe," she said in a soothing voice. The smile on her red lips almost hypnotized him. Aloud, her voice had the same sound as the psychic voice in his head. "Catch your breath. You are under my protection, but be cautious because I am under no one's protection," she finished with a hint of irony in her mysterious smile.

He sat up, but cowered slightly as he sized her up. She had an M-16 strapped on her back and an ornate sword in the scabbard on her hip, but no weapon in her hand. She was well aware of his distrust, but she seemed to have the confidence that she could handle him without the weapons if he tried something. That actually terrified him more than if she was locked and loaded for a war against him.

She said, "Morning is dawning and that is your time, not ours, but you mustn't go back to your village. The Specter controls those who lead it, as you already know and they will kill you, but before they kill you, they will get you to betray me."

Douglas started to protest, "I thank you, I would never betray you."

"They have ways that you can't imagine. You must understand my predicament. It would be better for me and make my life much easier if I simply killed you."

He recoiled slightly.

"Don't worry, I have fed already. You are safe from my desires, for now."

A rustle of leaves startled him, and he saw a squirrel bound by and she cast it a glance. Douglas saw it freeze like he and his three fellow soldiers had been frozen by a psychic command. The animal hung rigidly, its claws biting deep into the bark of a great white oak tree at her shoulder level.

Douglas protested, "I need to go back to my town and warn—"

"No," Abigail growled fiercely. She drew her sword and Douglas found himself frozen in place, at her mercy again. She slashed her sword and it swung at his neck. He cringed, but it passed him by and decapitated the squirrel still clinging from the tree.

She picked up the body and turned away as she sucked the blood from the neck and then tossed the bloodless squirrel to him.

She squatted at eye level as she told him, "Eat this later. You'll need food, but cook this well before eating. You will be safe from catching anything I have."

"I could become a vampire if I ate it raw?" he asked. The craving for immortality burned in his eyes.

She saw this desire and slapped him hard across the face. She replied sharply with disgust at his desire, "Do not confuse arrogance for immortality. Besides, most people who are infected by vampires do not turn, but rather die of insanity."

"Why are you helping me?" he asked, rubbing his reddened cheek.

She didn't answer but gave him a handgun with a few loaded magazines. Going weaponless in the Forbidden Zone was a death sentence. "If you need to shoot a vampire, aim for the heart or head, preferably one shot to each target. We're very resilient. Just don't try to shoot me, please."

"You got it and thanks. Hey--" he started to say.

She stood up from her squatting crouch and said, "I must go."

"What are you?" he asked. Later he thought it was an odd question, but in the moment it was all he could think.

She squinted, irritated by the early dawn light, put up her hood, and donned very dark sunglasses as the sun now just peeked over the ridgeline behind her.

"Who are you?" he persisted.

She turned and walked away replying over her shoulder, "I am not a monster."

| 2 |

I watched six children playing within the semi-ring of the slain zombies. The diameter of the encampment was about fifty meters in a deep ravine with steep slopes on either side sandwiching a clear brook. The bodies of the zombies were stacked about seventy-five yards away in a semi circle where they fell. Only the near freezing temperatures kept the stench at bay. I envied the innocence of the children, but worried about their jadedness. Surrounded by death, they continued on with their childhood as they chased each other, squealing and laughing, playing a game whose rules I could not determine. It seemed that one child ran with a stick as the others chased him until he was tackled. Then the tackled child tossed the stick and the other kids struggled to get it, and then the winner was chased until tackled.

With the point of a machete, Bryan had drawn a line in the leaf litter and dirt as the boundary for the children at twenty-five meters from the bodies. About five camp members had the double job of moving the bodies further away and keeping an eye on the kids, but despite the childlike desire to explore the boundaries of rules and danger, the children stayed another ten meters away from the line. The brutality of the punishment meted out probably kept them in obedience. Logically, I understood the necessity for a spanking to keep the children from getting bit by the undead, but my yet civilized mind found such strict discipline abhorrent.

I noticed the kids played nicely enough, but their shoulders were raised and that drove them, hunched forward in an aggressive posture. Both girls and boys, except for one lone child. He was a fair haired boy with wide thoughtful eyes that seemed both to take in information and reflect all his unconditional love.

I remembered that his name was Bradly, and that he was Bryan's oldest son. I instantly liked him and worried if such a thoughtful child could survive in this land without turning bitter. If he would survive, would he lose his openness in the process?

I stood still watching the child when a tribe member, who I didn't recognize, gruffly said as he passed by me, "You better go eat."

I nodded and arrived at the fire. I sat down on a log and looked at what was cooking. There was nothing but deer meat searing on a grill above the flickering coals. I didn't want to catch the hell I caught yesterday when I told them I was a vegetarian. Besides, I didn't want to eat the acorn gruel that they fed me yesterday either. I steeled myself to eat the venison.

Scott, the chubby older guy and incessant smartass, was grilling the meat. His ball cap was tipped even more to the side than usual. It seemed to say, "Yeah, I'm an old redneck and to hell with fashion statements," if he even knew what a fashion statement was. He looked goofy but that hid a former Marine who was deadly in a fight.

"Did you want your chicken feed for breakfast?" he asked with his ever present silly smile. The boiled and dried acorns were usually reserved for the egg laying hens through the winter months when the natural occurring food like worms, nuts, berries and greens were scarce.

My body was cold, exhausted. My overused muscles and sinews seemed to cry out for muscle and sinew for food. Deep inside, I really did feel like I needed to up my sustenance for the new life I was living. I also craved something else that I could not place my finger on.

"Give me the venison. I will eat like a lion today," I said.

A few people behind me, of whom I had yet to make their acquaintance, cheered my decision to eat meat. It irked me that my lifestyle was known throughout this village of tarp hovels.

"Wise choice, my man," said Scott.

I held out my metal camping plate. Everyone had their own plate and utensils. There may have been communal meals at times, but washing dishes was an every man for himself kind of chore. If you were too lazy to wash your plate, you either had a dirty plate or you used your hands.

Scott slapped a huge chunk of meat on my plate.

I was famished, so I sat down and dug into the thick chunk. With my multi tool knife, I cut through the charred brown sinews and exposed the rare red meat underneath. I watched the clear red juice drip down the knife to the plate. I tried a piece, stabbing it with my knife instead of a fork. It was tough and chewy, but the salty juice of it touched off an atavistic hunger that I didn't realize that I had had. I tore into it and quickly gobbled it up like a dog fearful that another cur would steal its food.

"It's good that you are consuming meat. It is a whole food with all the essential amino acids and fats needed to survive the winter."

I looked up and saw Bradley standing before me. His shoulders were back and his arms at his side so that his chest was open to me as if his heart was his gift. I smiled, seeing that the nine year old boy genuinely wanted me to thrive. The deep pools of his eyes seemed filled with an inner light. I continued to eat as he talked about the value of meat from the perspective of a survivalist and a physiologist. Quite a few times he used scientific words that were almost over my head and it sounded odd coming to me in his young kid's voice.

I caught a glimpse of his father, Bryan, as he looked over the field of slain zombies. The war chief's eyes rose to the hills above and assumed a wistful, dreamlike quality, and I realized that Bryan was once the wide eyed, altruistic youth who resorted to savagery to save his tribe. I felt my chest tighten in sadness as I chewed my meat. Bradley's voice became distant words as I realized that I was once such a boy too, timid yet open rather than aggressively hunched forward. What would I become out here if I survived? I had lost a lot of that openness from living in the relative luxury in the safe zone. I wallowed and dwelled in my self-imposed misery. I still had some of that openness in me. I needed to keep my compassion but lose my weakness.

I wanted to fight for the love still remaining in myself, in Bradly, and in Bryan's heart beneath his savage exterior. I felt a sudden overwhelming desire to smash through the fence and march back to Washington DC and change the world, but that was impossible-- for now. Originally, I embarked on this journalistic mission to further my career. Now that seemed mundane. This now went far beyond me, but I knew I must plunge into darkness before I could see the light.

I realized that before I could stand up for anyone else, that I had to stand up for myself. Yes, it was prudent to keep quiet and observe, but I was almost killed last night by the vampires because Bryan insisted that I have a short sword. I needed to demand that I be allowed to protect myself, I firmly decided as I chewed my last chunk of meat.

I looked down expectantly. The plate was empty except for the red juices sloshing at the bottom of the plate from the rare cooked meat. I drank it and then still needing more, I looked

around to be sure no one was looking, and then I licked it up.
I looked up at Scott when I was done.

He read the request in my eyes, smiled, and cut me off another chunk.

"You're a great cook," I said.

"No, you're just hungry." Bryan laughed.

"Hey!" yelled Scott. "I'm supposed to be the resident smartass."

Bradley started to tell me more about the horrors of starvation, but his father said laughingly, "Go play, son." Then he
said seriously. "Go easy, Eric. If you vomit, you're just wasting good meat the kids could have eaten later." Bryan then left
like he was on a mission. He had a way of doing things without speaking or excusing himself.

"OK," I said to his back, not knowing if he heard me.

As soon as Scott plopped the next piece down for me, I
started cutting into it before it finished bouncing on my plate.
I told myself to eat slower.

"I thought that after the carnage last night the last thing
you'd want is that carnage that Scott cooks on your plate," I
looked up and saw it was Critter, the tall lanky woodsman,
who slowly, deliberately seemed to drawl that last quip.

Scott stayed quiet. I guessed that he was too busy cooking
to be a smartass.

I didn't answer Critter, although I did maul the question.
The meat in front of me was fresh, bright red and vital. Not
a rancid brown like that of the zombies. Somehow the fresh-
ness of the venison fueled my hunger.

Bryan reappeared and handed me a ceramic coffee mug. "Drink this."

I made a face as I sniffed the suspiciously sour smelling brew.

"Drink it," Bryan repeated. "It's apple cider vinegar mixed with water. It's supposed to be a cure all. However, the acetic acid will help digest the meat. You'll need to feel healthy for what's coming up later."

I cringed as I shot the drink like cheap whiskey, but it wasn't bad especially after chasing it with cold spring water that was collected upstream, far from any dead zombie remains.

"What's happening later," I asked through sour puckered lips.

"Immediately after breakfast, we're moving the bodies further away so the kids don't get hurt and to prevent spreading of the disease," Bryan answered.

"Why don't we move campsites." I asked. "I'd prefer not to sleep another night next to them."

"We will later, but for the time being, the near freezing temps will keep disease in check. Besides, we have wounded who can't move at this point. They need a few days to heal before finding a new campsite."

I nodded my understanding. There was no way that Peter could be moved with a shattered leg.

Bryan left me to finish my meal.

When I had eaten breakfast, I wiped my plate with sand and water at the creek with the other tribal members. It was still coated with a tactile film of deer grease, but soap was at a scarcity. If it didn't smell of rot, infection, or decay, it was considered clean. When it came to actual zombie contact, then it was met with gallons of a homemade sanitizer that was made of tannic acid from boiled acorns, multiple types of alcohols, and local herbs and spices, particularly garlic, very heavy on the garlic. People around here tended to smell like exotic restaurants.

I walked back to the communal fire and stood in the background as some tribe members discussed the plan of the day. There were probably twenty warriors in all standing around. When there was a pause in the conversation, I blurted out what I felt needed to be said.

"So when do I get a bigger sword?" I asked. It was a question out of nowhere, but one that had been on the tip of my tongue since the battle ended or really, since I was given the short sword to begin with, and Scott made an innuendo about it being related to my pecker size. Beyond that, if I was to survive, I needed a real weapon.

The camp quieted as they all looked at me like I had committed a blasphemy, and then they looked at Bryan who startled me when I realized that he was standing behind me.

The war chief said, "Really there's no protocol. It's based on when you can find, borrow, or purchase one. However, I'll give you one for free, once I feel like you've earned it."

"Earned it? What the hell do you think I did last night? I probably slew over a few hundred of those things." I said with agitation. No one, including myself, thought I could have sur-

vived that battle yesterday, but I did, in spades. I had training in martial arts before coming here and would battle with
padded swords, but had never been tested with actual razor
steel in a battle for sheer survival. I thought that I performed
well and that a warrior had been awoken inside of me. My
friends back home would have been blown away at what became of their mild mannered companion.

"And a vampire," said Scott, with that smartass grin back
on his face. "You 'Buffy the vamp slayer,' you."

Everyone laughed. They doubted my story which pissed
me off more, ironically, even if my story wasn't true, but in my
defense, I was still trying to figure out what had happened last
night. Everything that happened with Abigail occurred while
I was under her hypnotic spell.

"What more can I do?" I demanded.

Critter was smiling but there was a reasonable tone to his
voice, "Try facing one of the Low Boys, or any intelligent being that doesn't come at you like this." Critter walked at me
with his arms extended, tongue hanging out, and eyes crossed,
looking more like an idiot than a monster. He stupidly made
an, "uuhh" sound.

I realized that I was standing in an aggressive stance. I was
angry, but mostly I really wanted to prove myself once and for
all. I wanted to be taken seriously. I wanted the respect returned to me that I both showed and had for all the members
in this tribe.

"Draw your sword," Bryan said as if challenging me to a
duel. He placed his hand on his sword, locked eyes with mine,

and drew it. As he did so, he took an ominous step toward me.

"What?" My hot head instantly turned to cold fear.

| 3 |

So far, I had survived for only one night what Bryan had lived through for two years. It was funny that I had not fully considered my request until it left my mouth, and now I had to deal with the consequences. Impetuous by nature, I hadn't been challenged when I lived in a civilized world. I had grown used to no one challenging an outburst, demand, or boast, but I quickly discovered that life in the Forbidden Zone had instant answers to my impulsive thoughts and actions.

"Draw your sword," Bryan ordered more firmly.

Now the camp was even quieter. Men and women grabbed their kids and scooted back to give room for whatever was to come. Adam watched from the background. He was the true leader of the camp. His seventy year-old eyes hid behind his reflective sunglasses. His body was impassive. Either he trusted that Bryan would not do something rash, or he really didn't care if I was killed.

I reluctantly drew my sword.

"Put it back," Bryan demanded.

I complied but with a questioning look on my face.

"Now draw it like you mean to slay me," Bryan ordered.

I obeyed and Bryan nodded with appreciation, "Your face looks almost mean. Now try to kill me."

I stood there. My feet froze to the ground. My hands held the sword at my waist with the point aimed at Bryan's face, but I couldn't move.

He shook his head. "This isn't fair for you. You're afraid of killing me. Critter, get us a short shinai."

Critter quickly brought a homemade bamboo sword. Bryan received it with a bow and then smacked himself over the head with it pretty hard.

"You won't hurt me," Bryan said. "Now, put down your wak." Wak was short for wakizashi.

I put it down, received the bamboo sword and looked at Bryan.

As he started to say "slay me," I pounced at him to prove once and for all that I was a formidable swordsman. He easily dodged by stepping to the side as I swung down. I swung across at his head and he ducked by bending his legs into a squat, ready to pounce. Every evasion seemed to put him in an advantageous position over me. I brought the sword back to bring down on his head and he unexpectedly sprang forward so that his face was inches from mine. It was too crowded to swing the long weapon at him. He knew it and smiled at me.

I heard the rough laughter of the men around me as Bryan playfully swatted me on the butt. It didn't physically hurt, but the playful insult enraged me more. I desired nothing more in life at that moment than to slash that grin from his face. I continued to chase him with the bamboo sword. Whether I stepped forward into him or retreated back or to the side, it was like he read my mind. He seemed to move before or along with me, like a dance partner with psychic abilities. I could not slash, stab, or strike him in any way with the sword. He even read and ignored my fakes.

All the while, each time I missed, he slapped me across the face. He was playful at first when he struck me. It didn't hurt, but again it struck something deep inside that made me want to scream at him. However, each slap was harder than the one before. I could feel my cheeks reddening from the blows as well as my building anger, frustration, and embarrassment. The louder the men around us laughed, the redder my cheeks became.

The angrier I became, the more Bryan smiled and the more I wanted to end his ability to smile, but I couldn't. He was always just out of reach or too close.

He hit me hard enough to make me feel dizzy, but it threw me into a frenzy. I swung three more times and each time he responded with a harder slap, each time bending me over like a willow tree in a gale wind. An impulse hit me. I dropped my sword and shoved him in the chest as hard as I could. I balled my fists up and chased after him. I actually had him on the run.

He stumbled back a few steps, snapped his fingers as he pointed at my face, and said, "good."

"What?" I asked as I stopped in my tracks.

"When something doesn't work, you drop that tactic and take an approach that does work. It's not quitting if you win with a different strategy. In a life or death situation, don't be as inflexible as long as you were in this exercise. If something doesn't work, you have to switch strategies in less than a heartbeat," Bryan said with another snap of his fingers.

"Or your heartbeat will stop," Scott drawled.

Bryan picked up the shinai and said, "Now it's your turn to get in close." Without another word, he bopped me on the head with the bamboo sword to the laughter of the tribe. Again, he seemed to be one step ahead. Again, the strikes were playful at first. Again, that smug ass grin...

"Quit looking at my grin. You're getting crushed by your pride, not the shinai," he coached as he simultaneously hit my head.

Bop.

"Breathe," he said.

"Bastard," I breathed and realized I was out of breath.

Bop.

"You're still holding your breath."

Bop. This time it was much harder.

"No kidding," I said.

He kept hitting me at will, interspersing advice like, "Relax." "Don't flinch." "Step, don't jerk or jump." "Breathe." He finally made me laugh when he said, "Quit looking like you give a shit."

It all seemed counter intuitive, but every time I saw him doing anything martial, he was as relaxed as if doing a waltz. He sometimes would smile to get under someone's skin, but usually he just looked bored. When taking a kill shot, his eyes blazed like a predator's briefly on his otherwise impassive face.

He finally let me get in close, but somehow the "blade" of the bamboo sword kept insinuating itself between him and me. One time I punched at his face, and he moved the bamboo sword so the blade touched my wrist. If it had been a real blade, I would have totally filleted the skin off the entire length of my arm with my force of the punch as it slid against the sword. I cursed. I did that two more times in a row. Most of the damage that would have happened would have been self inflicted from the result of my own movement, rather than him striking me. I occasionally walked into the stab as he placed the point in my way. He also used his knees, elbows and the butt of the sword with infuriating accuracy.

Before too long, rage again pulsed through my veins. My moves became more powerful, yet telegraphed. His smile grew and my anger mounted.

Finally, as our sparring became intense, he tripped on a root as he scooted back. Something very primal took over inside of me. It was like I was watching myself from above rather than acting. It reminded me of that one time I hit a homerun in little league. As soon as the baseball left the pitcher's hand, I knew the ball was mine. The baseball felt so smooth going off my bat and over the outfielder's head. The whole time I just knew it was a home run and I hadn't felt anything as clean before or since. Until now.

My eyes tracked his head and my fist launched like a Tomahawk Missile as he bent over. I connected as cleanly with his head as I did the baseball. It would have knocked him out, but he literally rolled with the punch, going to the ground and tumbling.

I pounced like a lion, instinctively for the kill. As he tried to stand, I lit into him and he had no choice but to receive a fractured skull or roll some more. I caught a sliver of fear in his eyes as he rolled to one knee on the ground. He was solid. As I charged, he pointed his hand at my face and snapped his fingers.

"Stop!" he ordered.

He instantly took power over me as I came to my senses. I stopped and dropped my fist.

"Sorry," I said as I realized my intent.

"No! Never apologize to me when you do what is right," he said calmly, like he was proud of me for hitting him. He rubbed a reddening spot on his temple where I had cracked him with my fist.

He stood up and slapped me on the back like a brother. "Did you feel that moment before you hit me when you no longer felt anger, fear or anything, just certainty?"

"Yes, I felt--" I didn't know how to describe it, or rather I felt ashamed to describe it.

"Yes?" he prompted.

"I felt power," I said confidently.

"Yes, yes, yes. You now need to find your power without wasting your time in destructive emotions. Fear, anger, embarrassment, pride, only cloud over that true power. If you truly master that, you will be a better man than me."

"How?"

"Train as powerfully as you pursued me while slashing with the sword but be as relaxed as if you are slicing potatoes."

"OK." I said. It somewhat made sense, but also, it didn't.

"This is not some hippy dippy, new age crap. This is learning control over your mind. You kept getting smacked because you were so angry at my smirk that you couldn't think of anything else but humbling me. You couldn't strategize. That's why you kept doing the same thing and getting smacked down. Me tripping on the root brought you out of your knee jerk reactions. I became your prey rather than an enemy."

I didn't like how it seemed that he read my mind, but I understood it as him knowing the basic human condition. It wasn't knowledge of fighting, but the wisdom of psychology behind the movement that he attempted to teach. However a part of me still desired revenge against him. For that, I did not feel sorry until later.

"Don't get down on yourself," Bryan said as he patted me on the back again. "Adam thrashed me just as bad when I was learning."

Adam said politely. "I believe it was even worse. You are twice as pigheaded as Eric."

The camp laughed at his sagely deadpan delivery.

"Now," Bryan said, "you need to intensely slice and beat the crap out of those posts while you are relaxed."

"OK."

It was weird. I actually relaxed as I went to work with the short sword on the post. The blade bit deeper than I had been doing the day before, but it slid out easily as I slashed. Chips of wood flew from my strikes against the wood. My body was sore from the intense combat of the night before, but the movement loosened me up very quickly.

As I was working on the posts, focusing on short swings and blocks combined with power, I noticed a pot of coffee percolating on the fire. I went to the communal fire for a drink after a few people got a cup.

I poured some weak coffee that was about 80% dandelion or some other bitter root to stretch out the foreign caffeinated bean. Yes, it was weak, but it still had enough of the magic in it to feed my addiction. I emptied the last of the pot and mindlessly placed it back on the fire as I was distracted by the work going on in the camp. I tended to do stuff like that. My parents used to get on me for putting empty milk cartons back in the fridge.

I watched the men moving the bodies of the slain zombies as I sipped the hot brew on the cold morning. As embarrassing as it was getting smacked around in front of others, I was grateful that they saw me as such a weak link combatively that they had me smacking a post around instead of moving zombie bodies that oozed vile smelling fluids.

As I sipped, making an awful face, I saw Robert and Tomas stop at a zombie body. They were looking at each other, joking about something that I couldn't hear. They had insufficient Hazmat gear, but it was all we had in the wilderness. Plastic bags wrapped around their regular boots. They wore industrial yellow rubber gloves that reached up to just below their elbows. I wondered why they would take such precautions this morning versus last night when they were covered in zombie goo and ickiness from boots to hair. The violence of slashing and hacking a zombie is quite a horror show. The answer had to be that last night they had no choice. This morning was the clean up after the party.

They bent to pick up a body, still distracted with their conversation. I swore out loud as I watched the body's bony hand reach up Tomas' arm. It grabbed a hold of his shoulder. Tomas screamed and recoiled in horror, but not in time. The zombie pulled its head up and bit Tomas on his bicep.

Tomas swore, pushed the thing's head and arm away in sheer terror and disgust. I saw a chunk of Tomas' flesh in the thing's mouth.

He jumped a few times holding his arm, swearing like I have never heard a man swear before. The terror laced shriek was even more shocking than the actual words. A dark awareness of his mortality smoldered in his eyes. A few men around us drew their swords, but kept them at their sides. I wasn't sure if it was to put Tomas out of his misery or just a response to alarm. He glared at me for a moment as if blaming me for attracting the horde in the first place.

A red haired female warrior stabbed the zombie through the head, ending its reaching arms and snapping jaws.

Tomas then addressed the whole camp as he screamed, "Kill me, now!"

I closed my eyes as he repeated it a few times.

Robert drew his sword to comply. He probably would have, had not Bryan approached. He placed a calm hand on the shoulders of the two men and said. "Put your sword away, Robert. Tomas, you may have an immunity for all you know. Let us wait."

Robert gratefully resheathed the sword.

Bryan amazed me. He could be the fiercest warrior or the gentlest negotiator. He could go back and forth as needed in an instant. The only ones who were better was old Adam and Shelley the herbalist, who quietly stood behind him.

Scott stood behind Bryan as well. He had also changed to a serious side that I hadn't yet seen, nor thought capable. Fighting for your life was one thing. It was the warrior's way, but waiting for disease to strike yourself or a friend was like helplessly dying of old age in a matter of hours.

Tomas nodded, but there was a hopelessness in his eyes. No one had known anyone to survive the bite. There were rumors of a friend of a friend of a distant cousin in a distant tribe who survived, of course, but no one knew of any first hand accounts.

The ravaging fever started within twelve hours followed shortly by death and then zombism. Other rumors claimed some immune systems turned you into vampires or some other mutant like monstrosity.

"You will be taken care of," said Bryan.

"One way or another," Tomas said with morbid humor. "Seriously. If I turn, I want to be killed while I am still a man. I don't want my mind or soul tainted with the insanity. I don't want--"

Bryan interrupted his rambling with a pat on the shoulder.

"You will be taken care of," Bryan reassured firmly.

Tomas calmed, but he continued to make sure he was understood, "I mean kill me while I have sense. I want to die as a man."

"First sign of fever, I will slice you myself," said Scott. It wasn't said with cruelty, but with the assuredness of someone who would do whatever he had to do for his friend, including giving a quick and honorable death.

Scott and Tomas shook hands, "Just no stupid jokes as you slice me."

"You got it, brother," Scott agreed.

It was a bit much emotionally. I looked away to get my mind detached before the emotion showed in my eyes. Tears threaten to well up to quench that fire. It was then that I noticed that the empty coffee pot I had idiotically placed on the fire, flared red hot. Something took over in my mind as I had a flash from the past. I remembered from my time in South America how people would deal with infections spread by an insect. I grabbed the red hot pot by the plastic handle and instinctively raced to the center of the scene. With full force, my body hit Tomas as I slammed the red hot coffee pot against his bloody bicep. We rolled on the ground as I held him tightly to prevent his escape.

His curses at me were emphatic, he rocked my head with a few solid punches, and the pot was burning me as well, but I held on for about ten seconds with the red hot pot smoldering in his bitten wound. I smelled his burnt flesh and heard it sizzle as the wound cauterized. I could hear the men and women around me cursing. Rough hands pulled at me as Tomas beat my face with his bloody fist.

Finally I was forced to let go. Critter and Scott pulled me up to a standing position as Tomas and I faced each other. Two men held back his violence.

"What the hell?" Tomas demanded.

Tomas charged at me and broke from the men who held him, but Bryan caught and restrained him as his fist just missed my face. The rest of the camp had their swords drawn, ready to cut me down on the slightest instigation from me or command from Bryan or Adam.

"Hold on," Bryan said. The grimness in his eyes told me that my life and death would be balanced by the words I spoke in the following seconds. "Why would you risk death to assault a friend and then continue as he punched you?"

"Yeah, what the hell, man?" Scott agreed.

Everyone who wasn't holding Tomas or me had a blade out and pointed at my heart.

I wiped some blood leaking from my nose as I blurted out, "Zombie fluids are gooey, including the spit," but I was speechless after that as I was panting after the grappling between Tomas and me.

I stood looking around, still a bit confused. Burning Tomas was exactly that feeling of power, the same compelling impulse when I punched Bryan when he tripped over the root during the sword drill earlier in the morning.

"What the hell are you talking about?" yelled Tomas who was still at the edge of Bryan's restraint.

I finally got my head together and replied, "It may be slow to infect. I was in Central and South America as a reporter. There was a bug that carried a disease. If bitten, people would immediately burn the bite with red hot steel to prevent the disease from taking hold. It worked, but time was of the essence."

The men surrounding me lowered their swords slightly but only slightly. The camp was silent.

"Dagum!" yelled Scott. "Don't a patient need to sign an informed consent form?"

Tomas was the first to laugh, though his teeth gritted in pain, "If it works I will thank you, but first offer a man a drink of whiskey before burning his flesh."

Shelley, the camps' herbalist and one of the camp's elders, pushed her way through. Sometimes what she said was held as law. I didn't quite understand the hierarchy, but it seemed to be based on which person spoke the most sense in the moment. She scolded us, "You men are crazy."

She made Tomas remove his protective hand from the wound. "Poor Tomas," she cooed like a grandmother. "This will make it feel better."

She rubbed some kind of balm she made with bear fat and local herbs into the scorched and bloody wound.

Tomas cringed as she applied it, but as the balm took effect he relaxed. She then wrapped some gauze, made from sterilized/boiled rags.

"Thanks, but could I still get some whiskey?" he asked.

"I have a good tincture that has healing herbs in it," Shelly offered. Tomas still looked skeptical. "It's made with 80 proof vodka," Shelley added dryly.

He frowned as if considering and nodded agreeably. "Then what are you waiting for, ma'am?"

"And sorry about this, Tomas," said Bryan, "but we need to tie you to a tree in the case--"

"I know the protocol. I would just prefer not to be in the center of camp. I feel like the criminal in the stocks in the middle of the village square for humiliation." Tomas said. I could see something was haunting him. I guessed it wasn't just fear, but a shame that went with an infection. I guess it's sort of like the labeling of lepers as unclean in Biblical times.

I watched them lead Tomas away. All the attention was on them, but I caught Bryan's eyes. He nodded, "You impress me. Now get ready we need to go soon. Be sure your sword is resharpened after swinging it against the post. You will definitely need it."

I nodded.

Bryan added. "You'll most likely get a chance to earn a longer blade."

Moments ago, passing that test was what I wanted. Now, that suddenly worried me.

| 4 |

Craig's hands shook as he rested them on the table next to his gun and the unknown drug that held him in an addict's cage. He closed his eyes against the weak man that he had become.

His mind overwhelmed him with a sense of urgency as the withdrawal symptoms kicked in and his desires wavered between ending the pain with the drug or the bullet. Sweat ran in rivulets from his shaved head, down his hard face, and into his long braided and beaded beard. His powerful hands kept trembling slightly as he gently opened the small white paper envelope that was similar to a salt packet commonly seen at a fast food restaurant. There was no writing that would give any clue as to what the white powder was that it contained. He carefully poured it into a silver goblet full of honey colored wine that sat on his mahogany desk next to his 1911 model .45 caliber handgun.

He sighed and relief washed over his granite face when the task was accomplished and none of his precious powder was spilled from his tremor. He swirled the contents and watched it dissolve. He stopped and placed the goblet back onto the table. As he looked at the mixture, his flinty eyes softened and then moistened. He placed his head in his hands and wept. This morning he had sent good men to their death with The Specter.

Craig sat alone in his office, a room in a historic mansion replete of southern gothic splendor. He was the ruler of his namesake Craigsville, home of the Low Boys as the Mountain Warriors called the people of his town. He longingly looked at the glass of wine that had dissolved the unknown drug that kept him enslaved to The Specter. He then looked equally desirous at the .45 handgun. One bullet would end it all.

He was once fearless. A warrior. Armed with a rifle and unyielding courage, he led special forces operations in far flung exotic regions of the world. Now he was effectively a slave to The Specter.

He picked up the gun with shaky hands and dropped it back on the desk with a rough clatter like it had turned into a serpent. He cursed himself for dropping his weapon. It was unheard of in his past life. Dropping a weapon affected its aim and that could affect his life expectancy in this crazy world.

Again his head collapsed into his hands, and he wept. Every nerve, cell, and fiber in his body screamed in torture. With each second that he refused to drink from the cup, the pain seemed to increase exponentially. He knew from experience that within a few minutes he would writhe on the floor in pure agony from the withdrawal symptoms.

Deep in his heart he believed that he would burn in hell for eternity in never ending pain if he were to accomplish his desire with the gun. Although he feared the never ending torment, he could not imagine how the torment could be any worse than the withdrawal symptoms from The Specter's poison. Craig actually began to fear the devious nature of manmonster more than all of hell's demonic forces, but one sip of the wine would begin to lessen the pain. To finish the glass would bless him with the feeling of an immortal if for only twelve hours. Maybe this time he would discover a way out of the addiction before the agonies returned, but this had become his daily ritual.

He picked up the goblet and swirled it around again and studied the light whitish sediment of the drug at the bottom of the cup of light golden wine. He could feel his eyes almost glow with desire like those vampire things when they were hit with the urge to feed on human blood.

***

In Afghanistan a few years before the quarantine, a sniper's bullet shot through Craig's leg and shattered his femur bone, shattered his military career, and shattered his life. The doctors reinforced his bones with titanium rods. To deal with the pain of screws drilled into his skeleton and mental demons, they gave him prescription narcotics. The pain medication gave him the ability to bravely relearn to walk. This seemed odd to a man who seemed unstoppable in the past, who could run three miles in under eighteen minutes at his prime.

Once back home, the prescription painkillers ran out, but he found the need went beyond the pain. The addiction became a being of its own. A constant companion like a pet that needed regular feeding. He soon became a functional addict. He was an independent contractor and a carpenter by day and ran a martial arts studio in the evening. He managed to keep it all together with a number of different drugs acquired through various services, both somewhat legit and straight up illegal.

When the southeastern United States was quarantined with the outbreak of the zombie disease, and Craig could feel the jones smack him for something, the man in the skeletal mask appeared from a Blackhawk helicopter. The Specter had all the power that Craig himself had once wielded overseas as well as the air of mystery. It was also obvious that in the Forbidden Zone, The Specter had no restraint on the death he could dish out. Unlike in regular warfare, there were no overseeing governing bodies that attempted to ensure a fair fight. The remaining population in the Forbidden Zone were officially considered dead, so they received no quarter if they went against the power that be.

The Specter had originally approached Craig with the offer to aid him in beating down the local resistance. Craig would be in charge of the entire southern Appalachian region. To end the meeting in agreement, The Specter poured some wine and toasted their partnership. Craig hesitantly brought the glass to his lips.

Why the skull mask, Craig asked himself.

Something wasn't right. Craig noticed a speck of white sediment at the bottom of the glass with that first toast, but he drank the sweet and slightly bitter brew so as not to offend his guest and new benefactor. Almost immediately, Craig felt clear headed, virile, and energized like he hadn't since before the leg wound and the subsequent addiction. Craig credited it to the vigor that comes with power. His head rushed with the responsibility to command again like he did in his prime. Except this time, it wasn't small units but rather a whole region.

For the first time in a long while, Craig had no desire for any drugs. Even the wine that he had with The Specter was very little, more like a ceremonial amount rather than enough to even make him lightheaded. Immediately he felt an intense loyalty to The Specter, a new ally who had enough faith in him to give him such a responsibility. Craig finished the glass and again noticed some residual white sediment at the bottom of the glass, but didn't give it any further thought in the moment.

Originally, Craig saw The Specter as providing back up to his force. The Specter operated secretly behind the scenes with men, resources, and most importantly intelligence that was headquartered outside the Forbidden Zone.

However, The Specter's knowledge wasn't limited to just the regional squabbles, The Specter uncannily knew all of Craig's quirks, sometimes seemingly better than Craig knew himself. In fact, as time went on The Specter would come back whenever Craig's confidence waned. A quick toast with The Specter's golden wine coincidentally gave Craig back everything he desired.

A week after the first toast with The Specter, Craig felt his old desires for narcotics, cannabis, almost anything reappear, but he knew none of that would satisfy him. He found himself desirous of The Specter's wine. He stared into the night out his office window as if searching for a fleeting answer.

As he pondered, insecurities began to plague him. Indescribable pain slowly started to flood his veins. However, his heart seemed to leap with joy as he heard the soft whomp-whomp of a distant Blackhawk helicopter. The sound of the chopper brought nostalgias back from his days as a leader overseas to the present day as he awaited his mysterious friend. It brought him back to the days when a helicopter arriving in a battle zone was his limousine ride out of a hellhole to the safety of home.

Out the window, Craig watched The Specter dismount the helicopter through the cargo door. He leapt out and landed confidently on strong legs. Following him were six people in the same black hooded cloaks as The Specter. The rotor wash thrashed the hoods of their cloaks. Something about The Specter's companions struck fear in Craig's heart. From the distance he couldn't quite put a finger on it. They looked oddly pale but vital, and yet famished. Craig feared the town's people would witness these odd visitors, but the townies knew to shut themselves up and hide whenever a Blackhawk descended. Or so Craig hoped.

Despite his trepidation with the new guests, Craig was prepared to greet them. However, The Specter dismissively pushed Craig aside and entered the historic mansion as if he owned the place. Craig could only stand and watch as the six, black robed figures followed with an air of ownership into his place as well. The Specter led the way to Craig's office.

Craig opened his mouth to protest but froze as he got a better look at the six visitors. He didn't know how, but he instinctively knew that they were vampires. It wasn't necessarily their pale skin, their dress, but rather the hunger for his blood or any human blood that fired in their eyes. Under their hoods, only their eyes were visible and they seemed to blaze with actual bloodlust. However as the only human in the room, and at this point he doubted The Specter's humanity, Craig had their undivided attention. Any soaring impulse of power that The Specter had inspired in the past evaporated like dew in the August sun. Craig actually found his gaze lowering submissively beneath the gaze of The Specter and his six associates, but it wasn't just submission. He felt ashamed at his new found alliance.

Overriding his shame was a fire-like needling in his flesh that wormed its way into his entire body. Craig needed something to ease the pain.

"Bring me the prisoner in the basement cell," The Specter ordered Craig's guard who stood outside the office.

The guard snapped a salute as if Craig himself issued the order and replied, "Yes sir!"

Craig was about to protest the usurpation of his authority in his own office, but he found his sweat dripping down his face blurring his vision. The needle-like pain that irritated his veins now felt like swords plunging into his organs. His head whirled like the planets and he suddenly found himself crashing into a chair.

The vampires watched him in patient silence.

The vertigo and pain washed over him and broke like a rogue wave. Craig stood back up, squared his broad shoulders, and demanded from The Specter, "How did you know I had a prisoner and how did you know that my holding cell is in the basement?"

"Quiet," The Specter boomed.

Craig's muscles writhed beneath his skin as tortured snakes. He tried to ignore the pain that built inside coming on like a tidal wave about to swamp him. He had to regain control in his office or he felt that The Specter would forever dominate him or worse, feed him to these beastly hooded vampires.

Through the fog of pain, he shifted his stance to face The Specter as if preparing to fight.

"Do you have an objection or something to say, human?" The Specter said "human" as he would scornfully call someone a worm.

Craig's head spun even worse than before. He grasped a hard mahogany corner of his desk and stayed erect as his body swayed. Craig felt the intense stares of The Specter and the vampires. The wave of pain that shot through his agonized body crested higher than the last time. His lips moved but he could not put his voice to his thoughts. His pain became his world. His present situation and those in his office disappeared from his awareness.

"Yes?" The Specter asked as his deep laugh rumbled and echoed through the mansion. Behind the skull mask, his eyes held the arrogance of someone whose plan was going perfectly.

As the pain lessened and the peak of torture passed, awareness of the situation returned to Craig. He started to speak, but a pounding at the door interrupted him.

"Come in sentry," The Specter ordered Craig's soldier.

The soldier obeyed and immediately opened the door pushing the prisoner before them.

The prisoner was a man in ragged clothing whose cheeks sunk from hunger. His last name was Connors. His family had resided in the area from the time when George Washington commanded the Revolutionary Army. Craig didn't know him well but had seen him around town before it all went down. In the before, Connors was a somewhat high ranking government bureaucrat, state or city, Craig didn't know or care. The post apocalypse world wasn't treating Connors well. He had dropped well over fifty pounds in the last year. He had spent the last two days in his cell for stealing eggs from a neighbor's chicken coop.

Craig wasn't sure of the man's fate, yet. It was in his hands to pass judgement. However despite running the town with an iron fist, Craig still had to behave like a politician. It was common for his people to shoot someone for stealing something as small as an egg. A child walked the thin edge of starvation, and the parents were ruthless. Connors was actually fortunate that he had ended up in the jail rather than facing immediate neighborhood justice.

The problem for Craig was that he didn't have the resources to feed prisoners, so Connors was facing either immediate freedom or execution, and despite depriving a neighbor of a meal (a capital offence), Connors still had many friends, some of them were Craig's soldiers. No matter his decision, Craig would piss off half of the town. There was no correct answer for the town's leader.

Both the guard and Connors looked with horror at The Specter. They relaxed only slightly when they realized that the hideous visage was simply a mask. However if he wore such a hideous mask, what unspeakable horror did it cover? That was the question in every mind that beheld the commander.

"You may leave, soldier," growled The Specter.

"Yes sir," the soldier said and gratefully left, closing the door behind himself.

"I am still in charge here," Craig said and cringed as he heard his voice crack like an out of tune saxophone.

The Specter ignored Craig and glared down at the convict who stood before him.

"He's emaciated. Hardly any nutrients in his poor veins," a middle aged vampire complained.

Connors eyes widened in terror, muscles stiffened from his planted feet to his twitching, hairless scalp.

"Richard," The Specter half growled and laughed at the middle aged vampire, "a mosquito should be grateful for whatever stumbles into its swarm."

Connors finally gained his speech, "I'm not sure what's going on, but you all have my solemn word that I will not steal another egg. I swear--"

"We are beyond that," The Specter said in a deep, soothing voice. Craig was surprised that Connors did not cringe but actually relaxed as The Specter placed a hand the size of a skillet on the condemned's shoulder. "We are beyond that," The Specter repeated.

Suddenly the masked creature grabbed Connors by the back of the neck and held him in place.

"Richard," The Specter said calmly.

Richard walked forward with a long slim dagger. Craig watched in horror as the vampires fed.

Even worse, Connors' piercing screams had to be heard by every living soul within a block. Craig watched as Richard rubbed Connors' chest in an almost sensual manner stopping the screams. Connors quit screaming and his eyes became distant as if hypnotized. Craig worried most that his soldiers would mutiny and depose him. The shrieks of the dying man seemed to trigger another wave of pain that shot through his body.

Craig realized that this was by far the most intense wave of pain that he had ever experienced, but it barely registered as he held onto the desk, mind numbed by the horror, but as the wave subsided and the vampires finished their meal, Craig mustered up every shred of courage he had. As Connors' lifeless and drained body was carelessly dropped to the floor, Craig set his jaw and said, "Specter! Our deal is off."

"You are correct," said The Specter. "There no longer is a partnership. You are now my puppet, and all your convicts now belong to our new friends," he finished as he motioned to the vampires whose lips were still red and moist with blood. "It is your job to find criminals to deliver to them."

Craig looked at Connors' body on the floor. The dead man's mouth and eyes still open in a final horrified scream. His face was pale and drained. Anyone seeing his corpse would know that he did not die of natural causes.

"Go to hell you masked freak! I only have to call my soldiers and within a minute, half the town will be here to slay you and these abominations!"

The Specter smiled at him as if everything was going as he preordained. Craig looked at the dead body of Connors. The horror etched permanently on the dead man's face was ghastly.

Craig continued when The Specter added no words to his smug smile. "I don't care if you wipe out this town with a swarm of strafing aircraft. I will die on my feet fighting you and them," Craig said as he gestured wildly at the six vampires.

The Specter continued to smile as he placed a wine glass on the table and produced from his cloak an antique blue glass wine bottle.

"I will not toast you, you sick bastard--"

The Specter's deep laugh rumbled and shook the building more than Connors had done with his piercing dying screams or his body's collapse against the oaken floor. The Specter poured the honey colored liquid into the goblet.

"I will not." Insisted Craig.

The Specter quit laughing. He was deadly prophetic when he pronounced, "Oh, but you will."

Craig felt a new wave of pain breaking on him. This was by far the most intense and he could tell that it was just building. Instinctively he knew this would take him to his knees.

He desired The Specter's wine, but even more he wanted to eliminate that deathly grin. He gathered himself, seeing through the blur of his sweat and pain as he charged the monster.

The Specter slid the rifle strapped to his shoulder to a more comfortable spot and easily stepped aside from Craig's wildly thrown punch and backhanded him, sending him slamming into a wall. The Specter then put his three hundred pounds of muscle into an uppercut into Craig solar plexus, lifting him off the ground.

Craig blacked out with a blink of his eyes and opened them to stare at The Specter's combat boots. He could smell the shoe polish. On the floor like a worm, Craig's fight was gone. Slowly, he looked up into the eyes of his master as pain wracked his body. He could feel every injury that he ever sustained. The inferno that was his femur felt as if the bullet had shattered it again, only this time the pain would not let him pass out but rather, it tortured him in its grip, forcing his senses to experience every demonic prod of hell. The torture inspired his mind to see blue electricity flowing around and entering his body. When he recovered enough from The Specter's blow and could take in oxygen, Craig begged, "Please."

The Specter smiled and picked up the wine glass and swirled the golden liquid. He studied it as if it were a prized possession. "I will make all your pain end."

Craig looked confused but hopeful.

The Specter mocked, "Do you really think it was your self empowerment? Your steely resolve? Your self discipline that let you give up your poisons? All your addictions to drugs? Your escapes?"

Craig just looked at The Specter. He felt as if worms had penetrated him like needles and swam through his body as easily as fish through water.

"Answer me, junky!" The Specter roared.

Craig couldn't answer. This wave of pain wasn't ending. In fact, Craig could tell it would only end in death.

"Please," Craig finally croaked. "Please." He hesitated and then begged, "Please, master, please."

The Specter squatted down holding his rifle so it didn't smack Craig as it swung around his shoulder with the displacement of his body position and weight. The man in the skull mask looked almost compassionate as he said "Over the last week, I have given you a potent drug that our labs recently discovered. It works as both a stimulant and a narcotic. A user feels invincible, but even better, the withdrawal is exponentially worse than heroin. Consider the pain that you are in, human. It will continually worsen over the next week. You will not be able to sleep nor pass out until the pain consumes you and you meet your death. I know you have some superstitious religious beliefs behind your lust for drugs and power, but do not expect any mercy from your God, because the pain will cause you to spend a week crying out every blasphemy imaginable. Do you wish to meet your maker when a curse against him is on your lips?"

Craig knew this to be true. He could only curse everything except the one person who could end the pain and that was The Specter. Craig wanted to taste that sweet and bitter wine. Tears streamed with his sweat.

"Drink this and your pain will end and you will feel your power," The Specter said soothingly as the vampires watched impassively with maybe a hint of disdain for their traditional prey.

The Specter lowered the glass to Craig's lips. His other hand grabbed Craig's shirt at his shoulder and lifted him up. Craig felt love for The Specter as he leaned into the goblet. The Specter pulled it away with a grumbling laugh.

"Will you do whatever I desire, human?"

"Yes! Yes! Please! Master," Craig pleaded, feeling like the worm on a hook.

The Specter placed the glass to his lips.

Craig gulped greedily. Almost immediately he could feel the pain subsiding. It came on like a wave. A new wave to counter the inundation of pain that had been wracking his body with regularity.

"Thank you. Thank you, master," he muttered over and over like a religious mantra.

After a minute or two, he realized he could stand again. Slowly he stood to his full height. He felt awesome again.

"Thank you!" he said reverently one more time. As Craig looked at The Specter he realized that he loved the skull faced creature.

***

That was a year ago.

In the present, Craig sighed and pushed the gun as far away as he could until it fell with a cold clatter from the desk onto the hardwood floor. He picked up the glass and drained it. He then wiped the sediment from the bottom of the glass with his finger and sucked it off with gratitude, relishing the bitter taste that brought such a sweet reprieve. He again felt love for The Specter. He was ready to conquer the world if his master decreed.

A soldier knocked on the door.

"One moment," Craig called.

He then picked up the small paper envelope and licked up the last bit of powder. The paper stuck to his dry, cotton feeling tongue.

Power surged through his veins as Craig boldly walked to open the door.

Craig didn't wait for the report from the soldier, but instead, barked to order, "Send the squad to the town to capture Eric Hildebrande."

Craig hoped that The Specter would be proud of him.

| 5 |

Even with the work performed, Bryan, Critter and I still set off to scavenge the local town before mid morning. The life around camp started as the sun arose. I guessed with the lack of electronic lights and LED screen entertainment, there wasn't much of anything to do but sleep from sundown to sunrise unless some pressing mission after dark took precedent.

As stiff and sore as I was from the combat of the night before and training this morning, I actually welcomed the trek. The first quarter mile was rough and then my body fell into step. Moving seemed to loosen every locked joint in my body and stretched every tight muscle. This morning I felt like I was half dead, but by the end of the first half mile, I was actually feeling fully alive and ready to take on the world with my new companions.

Critter led the way. He had an uncanny way of sensing what lay ahead on the trail. I followed in the middle and Bryan covered our rear. Without breaking stride, Critter would oc-

casionally point with his hiking staff at something that inter-
ested him without giving an explanation. Sometimes it was a
track, odd colored fungi, or something else I could see. Sometimes I could see nothing other than the brown leaves on the
forest floor.

I wondered about the wisdom of sending Bryan, the so-
called second in command, on this trek. Critter explained that
leading the defense of the village last night had pushed Bryan
to the limit mentally and this would give him a chance to un-
wind. At least it would get him away from the major causes of
stress-- endless politics and constant complaints of the camp.
Fighting zombies out in the woods didn't seem to faze him as
much. I guessed that was why he was quick to challenge me
this morning.

I had pondered his need to escape the politics of the camp.
I had read that people saw public speaking as one of their top
fears. I could only guess that leading a military assault/defense
was basically public speaking except if you failed, not just you,
but all that you loved would be lost. Literally, all would be
lost. Public speaking, on the other hand, was just the fear of
looking stupid.

Critter explained that a walk through the woods would
calm Bryan's mind. I resisted the sarcastic reply of, "A walk
through the woods in a zombie apocalypse." I guess getting
away from the carnage was a good thing even though I considered it as escaping out of the frying pan.

Zombies tended to prefer flat ground. As we entered into
the deep woods where he felt we were safer, Critter motioned

me to walk close to him as he continued to point to everything that stood out to an expert tracker, but now he felt free to give verbal commentary, as Bryan quietly covered our tail. Critter's eyes missed nothing from a bobcat's foot print to mouse turds. He explained natural connections that told the story of the woods. This story, that seemingly only he could see, fascinated him more than an old cat lady with her soap operas. Maybe that was because Critter wasn't a mere spectator of the woods. He was as much a part of the woods as the trees, the mice, and the bobcats.

We approached the town in the valley far below our trail and stopped at an overlook on our path and studied it. From above, with the parked cars around and the few residents wandering around the streets, it looked like the idyllic Appalachian small town. The winter grass didn't need cutting, so the town had a neat appearance. However the lurching shuffle of those current residents told a different more horrific story. We continued our journey.

When the trail approached the road that we would take into town, I stopped them.

"I need a number two toilet break," I announced.

"The men's room is behind that big poplar," said Critter as if he had a personal relationship with the stout tree.

"Thanks."

As I headed for the relative privacy, Bryan said, "We're going to recon the road. Just follow the trail down to us."

"I'm a big boy," I replied confidently.

They didn't respond other than give me a glance that betrayed their doubt. I went behind the large tree as they disappeared into the brush.

   ***

Tommy stared at his laptop's screen. A horrified intensity lit his face as he watched. The live scenes from the Forbidden Zone filled him with the same terror as if he was there. He couldn't imagine what his friend Eric went through dealing with the horror face to face. Tommy didn't dwell on that. The reason why Tommy's job was a bit easier than Eric's was strictly because Tommy was smarter.

Tommy currently resided in a building a few miles from the border and about eighty miles from Eric. Despite the security measures of a well-guarded electrified razor-wire fence, Tommy kept a helicopter on standby to whisk himself back to DC in the case of a fence breach.

The space in which he conducted his voyeuristic work was not quite as plush as his DC office, but he considered it a work in progress. Tommy actually preferred the nearness to the Forbidden Zone. He considered himself courageous for engaging in the fear of the close proximity. He also liked to have regular conversations with Don Renton.

Don Renton was a linebacker picked in the first round of the NFL draft straight out of college, but then all hell broke loose with the zombie outbreak. In that time he joined the Army Special Forces and quickly became a spook, almost literally. Where Tommy was the brains on the outside of the Zone, Don was Tommy's right fist on the inside. Don was one of the few people who could leave and enter The Forbidden Zone almost at will. Usually such a violation, either in or out, resulted in an immediate death sentence.

Tommy's clock chimed the ten o'clock hour. As soon as he thought that Don would arrive any moment from his latest incursion into the Zone, Tommy heard the helicopter. Looking at the bank of computer screens, he saw that it was Don's landing on the lawn. Tommy directed his secretary to send Don immediately into his office.

Tommy looked back to his laptop and flicked through a few dozen live footages sent in from the drones. He stopped as he watched a figure, hooded in a black cloak, walk through the woods. The eerie ability with which that the figure comfortably moved over the roots, rocks and changes in elevation almost gave the illusion that it glided.

Despite the covered features, there was something both feminine and feline about the hooded figure's grace. The confidence in her movement through the forbidden forest, creeped Tommy out. She was no mere person but rather a predator. He found a part of him both aroused by her gracefulness and repulsed by the fear of her.

Tommy touched a button and he heard the click of a solenoid and then the slide of a bolt as the door unlocked. Don immediately entered the room.

Without a greeting, Don walked around Tommy's desk and observed the screen.

"That's not just some weirdo, doomsday cult wannabe? That's an actual vampire, right?" Tommy asked.

"Absolutely," Don said.

"How can you tell?"

Don's chuckle sounded like the deep growl of a lion, "You just develop an instinct. I think you have it, but won't acknowledge it."

"I thought the vampires didn't like the sunlight?"

"They don't," Don said in his naturally stern sounding voice. "Hence the cloaks, sunglasses, and sunscreen. Even then they still don't like the daylight, except one."

Don looked closer at the screen, and cursed, "That's her!"

"Who?"

"The exception. Abigail," Don said, grumbling the name again like a curse.

"You know her?" Tommy asked

"Yes. She's trouble. She's got great promise. She showed far more psychic skill than anyone else even before she was turned. I don't believe she gave her full consent to be changed."

"What?" asked Tommy. "I thought if they were turned against their wills, they died of madness or were reduced to drooling imbeciles."

"We call those idiot vampires, 'faileds.'" Don replied. "She was turned on the brink of death after suffering a shattered leg and was delirious and gangrenous."

"How would she not go mad?" Tommy asked. The process of turning into a vampire was known in the scientific community to be maddeningly painful and in some ways scrambled or at least seriously altered the mind to be more receptive to psionic power. This change was confusing to all who suffered through it as reality blended with higher perception. In a dream filled delirium most people could not handle the sensory overload and succumbed to insanity and then to the numbness of idiocy if they survived.

"She's tough," Don stated. "Her power unlocked before Richard turned her completely. Her mind figured it out. It's believed that your friend Eric's mind is behaving similarly."

Tommy nodded, not surprised. He was in charge of the surveillance and entertainment wing. The science department operations were mostly kept secret from him. Don, although Tommy's underling, worked with both departments.

Don continued. "That's how she stayed sane. Her mind had already started the transformation process before Richard bit her. She dealt with the empathetic feelings and stray thoughts of others beforehand. She still shows great skill with the psionic abilities, but only when it slips out. No one knows her true skills or where her loyalties lay. She keeps a lot hidden from us. Most vampires see themselves as superior to people, she--" Don paused.

"Yes?" Tommy prompted.

"It's hard to describe. The other vampires have a pack mentality like wolves. She's like a lone wolf or a cat."

Tommy agreed with lust creeping into his voice, "She moves like a lioness."

"Yes, she's quite a looker. I actually liked her. She has a bit of spunk and is intelligent. I would like her more if she didn't interfere with our work"

"How does she interfere?"

"Odd things happen. I have no proof it was her, but-- You just get a feeling. However, I don't know if she has a loyalty to mankind or if she is playing a game with us. I sometimes fear she has indeed lost her mind and she saves people to spite us. She seems to have no regard for her own life, even. It's all a game to her."

Don paused thoughtfully and continued, "Another thing that's off is that she spends more time in the daylight than the others, and she has an uncanny ability to ditch our surveillance," Don said. "However, I think that she would respond well to a good slapping around. She'd have to be brought under our domination without stirring resentment and her rebellious nature."

They watched the black figure of Abigail move with a purpose. The sun blazed fiery behind her almost blinding the two men causing her silhouetted form to appear like an eerily shadow moving across the screen.

The hood turned its black maw toward the drone's camera. Tommy felt a shudder travel up his back. The shiver stopped at his shoulders causing them to bunch together.

"The drone is too far. She shouldn't see it," Tommy said as he worked with the controls and played with the close-up lens.

Suddenly, the color left the screen, changing to black and white. The images became spectral and stark, realistic and yet strange. Then the picture warbled and objects, like trees and boulders, appeared shorter and squatter and then taller and thinner, and went back and forth causing Tommy's stomach to churn. However, the female vampire remained unchanged, floating across the screen.

"That's what I mean," said Don. "The vampires have a small degree of mind control over people, but she seems to be able to tap into electronics. But brains and computers both emit an electromagnetic field, so theoretically if you can tap into a brain, you should be able to tap into a computer."

Don typed a few things into the keyboard and manually took control of the drone. He pulled it up and away from the dark figure.

As it panned out, the picture assumed more clarity. A few hundred yards from Abigail, Tommy saw Eric in the woods, alone.

"No," Tommy muttered with fear. It was obvious that the dark figure of Abigail headed straight for him.

The drone suddenly dropped and smashed into a tree and the screen went black.

Tommy moved to the computer and clicked a few more keys and tapped into the camera embedded in Eric's vest. Tommy screamed at the computer for Eric to hear him, of course without effect.

Tommy turned to Don, "She won't kill him, will she?"

Don swore at her and said, "She was strictly told not to kill Eric last night, but I think she has gone rogue."

"How so?"

Don explained, "She had to kill a human last night to prove her loyalty to the coven. Unwittingly they chose Eric. The

Specter stopped that. She probably wants to kill him now out of spite."

Tommy watched in horror as the black figure appeared in the range of Eric's camera. Tommy kept shouting helplessly for Eric to take notice.

Suddenly Eric's camera jerked as the body cam fully faced the black cloaked and hooded figure. Tommy breathed heavily as the dark maw of her hood focused on the camera, beyond the camera even, as if she had awareness of Tommy. She looked straight through his soul! Tommy screamed as the figure dissolved into blackness and flew straight at Eric and into the camera. The blackness flew through the computer's screen and attacked Tommy. He screamed again as his arms flailed to defend himself against her attack. Tommy had never experienced such terror in his life.

Don instinctively slammed the laptop closed with enough force to break the computer. Tommy came to his senses, and realized that he stood alone in the room with Don.

It was all an illusion.

"What the hell was that?" Tommy stuttered.

"Illusion," Don said grimly.

"How did she do that through the screen? Was that an illusion produced with the computer or my mind?"

"Maybe both. None of the other vamps seem to have that power, but her. Richard can mentally scroll through a computer screen, but we suspect that she can do much more. The belief is that there isn't much difference between the electromagnetic discharge from electronic equipment and an animal's nervous system."

Tommy ran his hands over his arms, chest and most importantly, his throat. He was almost certain that she somehow bit his neck. Once he was sure he was OK, he turned to Don and asked, "Is Eric OK?"

"I can't tell you that."

Tommy stuttered something unintelligible.

Don replied, "It would be safe to assume that your friend Eric is dead. He is no match for that vampiress."

"Can you terminate her?"

"I don't have the permission of the science department. They tire of her lack of cooperation, but they believe that she's more important than your show."

Tommy shot right back, "It's not a show. It's intelligence gathering."

Don laughed. "To the government it's intelligence, but don't try to fool me about your ambitions and intentions. The science department likes Abigail. She is far more important than Eric, for now. But if your friend doesn't get killed in the next few moments, we won't have to worry about her anymore if all goes as planned."

"Why is that?" asked Tommy.

"Because the science department wants to turn your friend Eric."

"Turn into what?" asked Tommy.

Don snorted and shook his head at the stupid question.

Tommy glared at Don. Tommy had always assumed that he was Don's boss, but Don had many masters. Tommy quickly said, "Eric's uncle is the Governor of this FEMA region. He would never allow it."

Don finally smiled back and said. "I gotta busy day ahead. I'll get my supplies and head back in."

When Tommy was alone he went to the computer. There had to be a way to save Eric. Don had his puppet in Craig, but Tommy had an inside man as well. Tommy feared the savagery in Don, but as bad as a friend as Tommy had been to Eric, there was no way he could let them turn him. He texted a message to his inside man in Craigsville.

| 6 |

I walked to the large poplar that hid me from the trail and took my squat. When I was done, I buried it after I wiped with a few big brown oak leaves from a nearby giant tree. Critter had just taught me that white oaks had rounded lobes on the leaves, where red oaks have pointed leaves. The white oaks were better toilet paper because they tended to be wider.

Aside from the hygienic aspect, another important difference in the two trees is that white oak's acorns were by far less bitter and much larger than red oak acorns. White oaks were where you could find more edible acorns and wild game for dinner. These were the type of acorns that they had fed me and the chickens.

I stood up, pulled up my pants, stretched and then on a bolt impulse, I drew my sword.

The tip pointed at the hooded cloaked figure in black standing ten meters before me.

"Abigail." I said. I was not able to see the facial features beneath the darken hood, but I knew.

"Short sword," she said in a deadpan voice.

"Are you here to make innuendos?" I asked, trying to figure out what she wanted.

"No," she said sincerely. "I worry about you."

"Worry? You tried to kill me last night."

"No," she said sweetly. "I was supposed to. I decided not to."

"Lower your hood then," I said shifting my sword.

"We don't like the sun, remember," She said as she brought the hood back just enough to see her face and eyes without exposing too much to the sun which was rising behind her. She started to smile. It brightened her face, but as it widened, I saw her twin, two inch fangs. She saw the sudden change in my facial expression and self-consciously covered her mouth with her hand.

"You are not a real vampire, just an infected wannabe," I said. I wasn't sure if I said this to reassure myself or to provoke her and show her that I had no fear of her. "I'm not afraid of you."

"Then why do you think about me all the time?" she asked.

I shook my head and resheathed my sword. I oddly felt confident. Besides her fangs, she looked like any other woman in the daylight, and with her weapons put away she didn't look dangerous at all. I remembered the usually fearless Critter blowing past all caution of using a firearm and drawing on her when he believed her dead at his feet, but I wasn't sure why he would take such precautions. I didn't know if she actually warranted it.

She laughed lightly. "Such a babe in the woods. You would not have put the sword away if you knew what I was capable of."

"The four of you vamps didn't kill me last night."

"I told you that I was supposed to feast on you last night," her eyes were soft, sincere.

"Why didn't you?"

"Besides the interference from The Specter, I couldn't."

"Guilt?"

"No, things weren't," she looked for the right word and settled on, "right."

"Oh, neuroticism then."

She shook her head, still smiling. "Don't mock. You may not be infected but you are, in a way, one of us."

I cursed her savagely and stated bluntly, "The hell I am one of you!"

"Your mind accessed ours. Most humans can't do that. Most vampires can't even do it as well as you," she said ignoring my profanity. "I can. You and I are rarities."

"That's crap!" I said. "You can't screw with my mind. I'm on to you." I didn't quite know what I was talking about nor why I felt suddenly enraged, but it was one of those things that I felt had to be said in the moment. Although I still felt under her spell, I felt like I was beating her at her own game. I could sense her mental probing and I felt my own mind psychically smacking her down. She herself had stated that I had some latent abilities. However, I still felt violated from her men-

tal probing, but I kept a firm facade. "You are nothing, vampiress."

Her smile widened as her eyes narrowed.

I closed my eyes and shook my head as if to clear a fog that
was threatening to descend on me.

When I opened my eyes, she stood inches from my face.
Somehow, I had briefly lost consciousness. Although she
stood slightly shorter in height, the slope of the hill had her at
eye level. Her crimson lips smiling in my face. I caught a whiff
of her faint, but intoxicating scent. So faint that I desired to
move closer to smell her. Underneath the natural perfume
was the scent of the forest soil, earthy with maybe a negligible
smell of decay as if she lived underground.

I stared for a moment as if hypnotized when the spell was
broken and sheer terror struck my heart. I fell on the ground
as I scrambled backwards, downhill from her. My hand spas-
tically slapping at the hilt of my sword, unable to grasp it in
my sudden panic and compromised position.

"Please don't mock me again," she said calmly with a be-
mused smile as she followed my retreat step by step in a delib-
erate, slow, confident walk.

"What the hell was that, that you just did?" I asked. "What
do you want?"

"Richard," she said. When I looked confused, she answered, "The older one wants you dead. I had to sneak out to
speak to you, at a risk to my immortal life. The higher ups
including The Specter want to infect you with the vampiric
virus. They want me to deliver your ticket to immortality.

They believe that the strain that infected me will make you the most... useful. But I want you to live as you are."

"How do you know that you're really immortal?" I challenged.

"Richard promised before he changed me," she said firmly like a true believer.

"How long ago?" I asked, keeping the skepticism from my voice so as not to offend but rather give her some self doubt. I slowly stood trying to regain my composure.

"A few months ago," she said

"So not enough time to know whether you are aging or not?" I asked. Once I was standing, I let the skepticism show. The way she had earlier covered her fangs told me she didn't want to be a vampire. If she had turned, yet had no immortality, it would rattle her and I was sure I could get more honesty from her if she wasn't so confident. In retrospect, I don't know if that was the wise course of action, but my head was swimming as if in a spell.

"Richard promised!" she shot right back

"Right," I said with heavy sarcasm, in an attempt to really shake her.

"You do not know what you are dealing with, Eric!"

I nodded, "And that's why I am asking you these questions. So if you won't tell me anything solid about you, why did you visit me, right now?"

She gave me that smile of superiority again, but her lips covered her enlarged canines. She said, "I have already performed my service to you while you blanked out a moment ago."

My hands instinctively went to my throat to see if I had been bitten.

She laughed, "No, not that. Not yet anyway. You may not survive to get it."

"Then what?" I demanded.

I heard footsteps lightly crunching the dry brown leaf litter behind me.

"Eric, what's keeping you?" Critter called from outside of my sight, hidden by the slope of the mountain.

When I didn't answer, Critter asked, "Do you need help wiping your own ass?"

I had almost forgotten who Critter and Bryan were. I felt my head spin. I closed my eyes and opened them.

"Eric. What's the matter with you?" Critter demanded.

I looked straight up at Critter from the ground. I must have fallen. Abigail was gone. I doubted if she was really ever there. Did I dream it all, I wondered? Critter looked over the forest floor and didn't seem to see any disturbances in the leaves that would betray her footprints. In the gloom of twilight, he had seen The Specter's boot prints last night. He should have seen Abigail's trail in the broad daylight. If he didn't seem to see her footprints, I started to doubt my sanity.

"I thought I heard something. Maybe a forest creature and I tripped," I said quickly.

"You were correct. I am the forest creature," Critter said, boastfully. He looked at me closer and asked, "You OK, man?"

I laughed louder than I should have, "I just took a big crap and slipped down the hill after I buried it."

"Uh, yeah. Get up. Let's go," he said.

Despite the vision of the vampire girl, I quickly forgot about the incident. The memory was dreamlike in quality. So it trickled out of my mind like sand through a glass until it seemed like it was gone. Entering a town where I had seen actual zombies took my full attention.

When we caught up with Bryan on the road, Critter and Bryan gave me a quick rundown with the mission. We were going to get a tarp, some antibiotics and painkillers for Peter, and different things.

"I hope coffee is in the 'different things,'" I said.

"I hope so too," said Bryan.

Critter shrugged. He was a true man of the woods. A bit of a practitioner of stoicism. He purposely did without pleasure and that included stimulants. I sometimes wondered if he found pleasure in the pain of life. The only pleasure I had seen him indulge in was to share the whisky bottle last night after the raging battle, but that was more built on the foundation of camaraderie rather than intoxication.

When I asked if there was a good chance there would be coffee, Bryan said this town was isolated in a cove and it was basically their town to scavenge. This was out of the Low Boy's range as agreed to by a treaty.

"So we're only looking at a fight with zombies, not people?" I asked.

"Yep," said Critter. His eyes were on the road ahead and the adventure that awaited. "But never take anything for granted."

That actually came as a relief. I faced thousands of zombies last night. I could face a handful today.

Critter explained, "So if we are downwind from a zombie, just shamble along. They pick up on scared jerky human movement, smell of human flesh, and of course, loud noises."

"Also they smell sweat, probably nervousness and fear," Bryan added.

"So don't sweat it," said Critter with a wry grin.

I shot back, "So I'm not supposed to get scared and sweat when a zombie tries to eat my brain?"

"Actually," said Critter like a professor, "It's easier to stay relaxed than to work on not being scared. Don't hold the muscles of fear."

"Which ones?"

"It's not the time for a damn lecture," said Bryan. "Eric just don't hold your shoulders up by your ears, let them hang loose and stand straight as if you rule the world" He mimicked a cowardly stance with his shoulders up by his ears and hunched over in a cower and then stood confidently. "We'll work on other stuff tomorrow in your training."

I just nodded.

"You take point, Eric." Bryan ordered. "Walk slowly. Listen, feel. If we encounter a zombie, it's your responsibility to kill it to save the group."

I stared at him wide eyed.

"Relax the shoulders," Critter instructed. "Feel how they are restricted in movement? That needs to feel foreign to you at all times. Your shoulders should float on the rib cage, not be welded to your neck."

Bryan slammed two hammer fists into my shoulder muscles almost dropping me to my knees as I felt lightning bolts shoot from my neck into my finger tips. I stood strong, but my muscles were temporarily too sore to bring my shoulders back up.

"That should help," Critter said.

I stared at them for a moment and when I found myself speechless, I laughed. Once the shock of the blow wore off, I noticed that my shoulders did feel more relaxed.

"Move," said Bryan. "You dwell on stuff too much."

I nodded and took point. Inside I was nervous, but I played confident.

It was odd taking point man in the patrol. I was trying to focus on everything I had learned all at once. Eyes open and take in the periphery—no tunnel vision. No daydreaming. No thinking of girls back home, or that vampire girl in the black hooded cloak who lived in the forest. Relax the shoulders. Walk quietly. Look confident so Bryan and Critter would not give me hell... My mind delved in a thousand directions at once.

We rounded a curve in the road and saw three zombies. They dully looked at me and walked towards me. I tried to avoid them by doing a zombie walk toward the other side of the road where a wall of a sheer cliff touched the pavement. The rock wall towered over a hundred feet above me.

I was really sweating it.

The three zombies zeroed in on me as I tried to play it cool like a zombie on a casual stroll.

They were twenty feet away when a light seemed to go on simultaneously in all three of their pairs of eyes and they took off in a sprint towards me with their savage growls. I kept trying to play it cool, still zombie walking away from them as they rapidly gained on me.

"Draw your sword, dammit!" Yelled Bryan as I kept the lurching walk that I was initially instructed to do.

I grasped the sword hilt. It barely registered to me that the handle felt different. I withdrew it, sliding the scabbard back and pulling the blade forward. Something was wrong. The blade was longer than I expected. I yanked hard and cleared the extra foot of the blade. It was a three foot long sword instead of my two feet long wakizashi. I didn't have time to ponder that this was not my sword.

I turned the drawing motion into a slice and decapitated the first zombie. The blade sliced through the neck much easier than I expected and slammed into the rocky cliff, making a shower of sparks. I used the rebound off the cliff to slice the second zombie.

My blade was stuck too far inside the zombie's ribcage to slash the third one. I froze in panic expecting a bite when the third zombie's head flew off as Critter's sword sliced through it.

"Dang, I thought you were never going to draw," he said.

"You said to play it cool," I said

"Play it cool, not stupid. When they're a football field away, you can just walk. You have to fight when you're already on their dinner plate," said Critter.

"And don't freeze like that. You need to relax," instructed Bryan, thirty yards away as he walked closer from the tail end charlie position. His calmness irritated me.

Always with the relaxing. I didn't answer. I was sick of being told to relax in a place where it was impossible to relax.

Critter continued, "That was good sword work once you got started, however, I'm surprised you didn't shatter your blade on that rock."

Bryan arrived up close looking suspiciously at the weapon that I still gripped and asked, "Speaking of swords, where in the hell did you get that beast?"

I suddenly felt the foreign handle in my hand. I had totally forgotten about it in the heat of the battle. I looked down and saw a large katana-like sword in my hands. At my belt was its scabbard, beneath that was my sheathed wakizashi.

"I—" I could only stammer.

"Let me see that," Bryan demanded and yanked it away from me. He studied it quickly and then glared at me. Although very utilitarian in use, it lightly resembled a fantasy type sword that geeks would display in their parent's basement room.

"This is a vampire's sword," Bryan said as an accusation.

"Oh," I said, thinking of the hooded figures in black from the night before. It did resemble the swords the four vampires had pointed at me.

"Let me see that," Critter said with the excitement of a sword fanatic.

"Where did you get this?" Bryan demanded.

I was too confused to tell the truth or even make up an answer. I stammered and only got out, "I-- I-- I--."

After a moment, Critter filled in for me, "He slew a vamp girl last night, remember?"

Bryan was very suspicious now. He got in front of me, eye to eye, "So you got this last night, and this is the first I have seen of this?"

I shrugged helplessly. I tended to speak honestly, not necessarily because I am always virtuous but rather because I am a poor liar. I can't hide it from my face, but in this case, I didn't even know what the truth was other than Abigail had just given it to me when I was under her spell, but I couldn't just tell Bryan that. He would suspect me of being bitten and infected or in cahoots with them.

Critter swung around the vampire steel, thoroughly enjoying it. "Sweet," he said admiringly as it whistled sharply through the wind. So enthralled was he with the blade that he didn't notice the drama between Bryan and myself.

"In case you didn't realize, Critter and I are knife and sword nuts. We'd have noticed this as soon as you wore it at your hip." Bryan then turned to Critter and said, "Let me see that thing."

"Where did you get this?" Bryan demanded again as he grabbed the sword from Critter.

I still was in shock and maybe still under her spell. I thought of Abigail standing before me. Her smile that seemed as bright as the sun that she hid from. The fragrance of her. The confidence of that woman. My loss of time when she was suddenly in my face. Was that the mission she fulfilled, to give me that blade?

"Where did you get this?" he repeated with much more force.

"Give me back my sword, Bryan." I said with an edge as sharp as the vampire's blade. I was surprised when I spoke so boldly, but I didn't show my surprise. In fact I felt ownership of the blade and I was even willing to fight Bryan for it.

Bryan glared at me. It was an impasse.

"The dude earned it, Bry'," Critter said. "He killed the vampire last night."

"Did he?"

"What are you implying, Bryan?" I rasped.

"That I smell bullshit somewhere."

"Give me my sword, Bryan," I growled.

"Come on guys," Critter pleaded.

Bryan stood his ground, "If you won it in battle once, you can do it again, right Eric?"

I was about to rise to the bait, but my aggressiveness melted into curiosity.

"Seriously, what are you accusing me of?" I asked.

"I don't know. Some things don't add up. When that happens in this land, people get killed," Bryan said. Then he held my sword in front of me teasingly offering the handle. I didn't bother reaching because I knew that he'd yank it away..

"What doesn't add up, Bryan?" I asked with the edge coming back into my voice.

Bryan got right in my face causing me to back up so that I was pressed against the wall of the cliff. "First off, what the hell are you doing in my tribe? Why weren't you dropped off with the Low Boys? Why not anyone else in the Forbidden Zone? Why are we so blessed with your presence? How do the vamps avoid everyone in our tribe, yet someone who can't fight, never even held a real sword came across this."

I started to object and he said, "Yes, I know you fought with padded swords. That impresses me as much as if you told me that you were a champion pillow fighter. Now you suddenly wield a real sword and you hunt down a vampire and kill him?"

"It was a her," I said.

Critter stepped in between us. "Bryan, relax. I saw the vampire chick dead with my own eyes."

"Did you see him kill her with your own eyes?" Bryan demanded with equal fury at Critter for taking my side.

"No," Critter admitted.

"Is there anything that could have killed her, a falling boulder, a stake flying out of nowhere," Bryan asked sarcastically.

Critter thought for a split second and answered, "I saw The Specter's boot prints."

For a split second, I saw a trace of fear in Bryan's eyes, and he stepped back from me. Always, he faced things with an almost fatalistic calm. Critter looked a little worried as well.

"Who or what is Specter exactly?" I asked. Although I had seen him face to face, I still doubted that he was fully human.

"Is he your vampire's slayer, Buffy?" Bryan said in a tone that was more accusatory than a question.

"Screw you, Bryan," I said as I took an aggressive step forward..

"Come on, get your sword, Buffy." Bryan said as a challenge. He held it out, daring me to grab it.

Bryan leaned aggressively towards me. I returned the aggressive stance.

No, I wasn't telling them everything, but dammit, not even I knew what the hell was going on. What answers could I tell them when I was searching for those answers myself? I was pissed off at that point. I had forgotten the thrashing that he had given me earlier to the point that I would gladly have taken another ass kicking than be called a liar.

Critter said with desperation, "Come on guys. Chill."

My blood seemed to freeze in my veins when I heard an unfamiliar voice say, "Yeah, guys, chill," in a stern but calm commanding voice from behind us.

Critter and Bryan reached for their guns.

| 7 |

"Remember, I said 'chill,'" the voice from behind us commanded.

Critter and Bryan froze and slowly removed their hands from their weapons and raised them to chest level. They wiggled their fingers to show that their hands were empty. I copied them. Critter had told me later that although it was a show that they were unarmed, dexterity in the fingers was that first thing that was lost when under stress. Wiggling the fingers brought control back to them and prepared them for a quick draw, if needed.

I looked over and saw five men spread out in a semicircle. They were much cleaner and better groomed than the Mountain Warriors. They wore tactical clothes that SWAT Teams wore and the uniforms were in new and freshly washed condition. They had tight haircuts under paramilitary caps and half the men were clean shaven. The ones with facial hair had trimmed goatees instead of the wild beards of the Mountain Warriors. All of them were armed with what looked like M-16s to me.

"What brings you around here, Josh?" Bryan asked as if Josh was his old buddy.

"Keep your hands where I can see them. All of you. In fact, lace your fingers on top of your head and kneel. Sanford is up above with his sniper scope. So don't get funny, especially you, Critter and Bryan," Josh announced.

"We're cool. Tell Sanford to relax, will ya?" Critter suggested.

"He will relax if you do as you're told," Josh replied professionally.

I complied. Critter and Bryan acted pretty confident as if this was a misunderstanding among friends and didn't obey Josh's command.

Josh lit a cigarette with his left as he still aimed the rifle with his right. Oddly It didn't seem careless to me. Josh handled the weapon as if it was a part of him. Josh repeated, "Sanford's mood is solely based on your cooperation. Don't do anything funny." Josh then repeated, "Now get on your knees and lace the fingers. Nothing funny."

Bryan said as he slowly knelt without placing his hands on the ground. "I'm not feeling very 'funny,' Josh. What are you doing over here? You're violating at least three tenets of our truce."

"Cuff them." Josh said.

"What the hell, Josh?" said Bryan. He started to stand, but when Josh kept the cigarette in his mouth and sighted on

Bryan's face with both hands on the rifle, he stayed on his knees.

One of the five men approached and tied Bryan's hands behind his back. I guessed that he was a former law enforcement officer from his professional demeanor and unencumbered manner in dealing with prisoners. "This is only for your safety and ours," he said as he tied Bryan up.

Bryan snorted in reply. With his hands bound there was a sudden, wild animal look in his eyes.

"So what's up?" asked Critter as his hands were tied.

When the man tied my hands, he did so with supreme confidence and used enough pain compliance by twisting my fingers to convince me not to do something stupid, yet gentle enough that I didn't panic and act rashly.

"We're here to pick up Eric." Josh said. As the ex-law enforcement guy finished tying my hands, Josh told him, "Don't bother tying the reporter. He's harmless."

The ex-cop let go of my hands and untied my bonds as Critter and Bryan glared at me. I stood.

"How did you know that we would be here with Eric?" Bryan demanded.

"The Specter told Craig to send us here," Josh said.

"Son of a bitch! You're working for the vampires and The Specter!" Critter yelled at me with more fury than Bryan had when questioning me about the vampire sword. He had stuck up for me and now he saw me as a traitor.

As the ex-cop motioned for us to stand, Bryan rocked himself from a kneeling to a standing position in a split second, and suddenly launched like a rock out of a slingshot. His shoulder caught the ex-cop under the jaw with the sickening sound of teeth clacking together. The ex cop went up in the air and crashed into the ground unconscious.

Then Bryan propelled himself into me, knocking me down. I slammed into the rock face of the cliff and crashed into the pavement. He stomped at my head and chest with the heel of his combat boot. I rolled back and forth out of the way. Each time his full 180 pounds crashed into the pavement with his boot heel either just missing me or glancing off of my face and body. I was sure that if a stomp caught me square on the head, I would quite easily die of a crushed skull.

He finally wedged me between his left leg and the cliff. I couldn't move. He raised his right foot and brought it down toward the stationary target—my face. I watched with horror, knowing that this was it.

Somehow his foot went limp and his entire body collapsed on top of me instead. Josh stood over Bryan with his assault rifle. The butt of it was held where Bryan's head had just been.

"Did you kill him?" I asked.

Josh shook his head and nudged Bryan off of me with the toe of his boot, "No. Most likely not. His skull is too thick. I just rifle butted him. Although, he will wake up with quite a headache."

"You're a dead man, Eric," Critter said in a tone that wasn't bravado. It was a promise, a grim prediction.

"I'm sorry. I don't know what's happening," I said in a pleading voice.

Critter looked away. I think he wanted to believe me, but hell, I wouldn't have believed me if I were him or Bryan.

They shook Bryan awake as they readied to leave. He was dazed but his eyes blazed at me and Josh. The way that the back of his head bled, I could tell he was in pain. That pain and hatred is what manifested at me through his eyes.

Josh's crew roughly pushed Critter and Bryan along to get them to move. However, they politely motioned me to follow.

As we started walking I said, "Excuse me Josh, or sir."

"Josh is fine. What's up?" he asked

"I know you're here to get me, but could you either let these two friends of mine go or at least be nicer to them?"

"They don't act like friends," he said with a rough laugh.

"Still..." I said.

"Listen," Josh said politely but firm. "You mind your business, we'll mind ours." When I didn't answer he said, "Understand?"

"Yes sir, but why are you taking them if you want me?"

"The boss wants to renegotiate the truce with that group up there. Catching the second in command is just a bonus. Also, we could always use a tracker like Critter." He then leaned in my ear and whispered, "Keep quiet, but Tommy wants me to protect you."

I felt a slight sliver of hope swell in my chest.

Bryan and Critter trudged along in their brooding. The strong silent type, I thought.

"Why do—" I started to say.

"Why don't you shut up," Josh hissed. "Creatures have ears."

I noticed that Josh and his men were alertly scanning the area around them. They were strong and silent to be more attentive, I decided. Listen more, talk less, was some good advice from journalism school that applied for survival as well. Especially for survival.

Bryan finally spoke up, "If we're going to your base, why are we headed this way instead of toward the trail?"

"We'll all ride in style today, boys," Josh told him.

Critter looked impressed for a brief moment.

Bryan then proposed, "If we're going to renegotiate the truce, why don't you make an offer of goodwill and untie us and give us back our weapons in case we're attacked. We'll go to your town peacefully, you have our word."

Josh snorted and shook his head no.

Bryan didn't persist.

Josh pushed Bryan and Critter a few steps ahead of the group to keep them covered. It seemed funny that these armed and obviously tough guys were still nervous about Bryan and Critter despite being tied up, outnumbered, and outgunned.

When we turned a bend in the road, the town came into view, as well as two zombies. Those two had that dull look in their eyes until they saw us. It was weird, they were actually wearing nice, new, and oddly matching clothes, blue jeans and denim shirts, not the rags that had survived two years in a post apocalypse zone. Their skin was smooth and not diseased or ragged. However they were still dead and grey. They looked like twins.

Then something seemed to suddenly click inside of them. They charged at us. There was no lurching or shambling. It was a warrior's charge. Each had matching hatchets in their left hands. Despite the thousands that I saw last night, this was the first time I had seen any of them armed with weapons and they raised them like they knew how to swing them. They snarled loudly and charged straight for Bryan and Critter as the armed escort and myself backed up. With their hands tied, I cringed anticipating the obvious outcome for them.

The first zombie reached Critter and swung the ax straight down at his head. Critter stepped to the side at the last moment and kneed the zombie in the belly. The creature bent with the impact and its own momentum. Critter slammed his knee into its face. Next he used the same foot to stomp its knee. The creature's leg collapsed. I cringed. I had never seen or heard a leg snap like that.

The creature still crawled after Critter. It swung the hatchet causing sparks to fly off the pavement. Critter stepped forward and kicked the head like a punter would a drop kicked football. The zombie was raised off the ground and collapsed. Critter stomped its head into the pavement before it could rise again. It lay still with its stinking, rotting brains leaking from a shattered head.

The other zombie swung across, straight at Bryan. He had no choice but to drop to the ground beneath the arch. Without the use of his arms, he slammed on the side of his shoulder against the pavement. As he did, his legs scissored the zombies knee, forcing it down on the road with him. Bryan then slammed the heel of his boot in the thing's head.

It moved toward Bryan and swung the hatchet causing Bryan to roll. Its hatchet sent sparks off the pavement, too. Critter stood on the thing's ankle to stop its movement. Bryan rolled to his side, into a crouch and onto his feet. He kicked out the zombie's supporting arm. As its face hit the pavement, he stomped its head in the ground in a similar manner to how he tried to stomp on my own head..

"...and that's why you gents are staying tied up," said Josh.

"Dayam! I thought you guys were dead," said the ex-cop.

"Yeah, thanks for the help," Bryan said sarcastically.

"Yep, they got out of our way so we could work," Critter said with deadpan sarcasm.

"Quit complaining. You guys handled it well, and you know it," Josh said.

"What the hell were those things?" I asked. "They looked like twins."

"Probably clones," Josh said.

My mind was blown. Who would clone these beasts and for what purpose?

Even Critter seemed concerned, "Really? I've never seen them with axes. Sometimes they might carry something, but they have long forgotten to use whatever it was. I've actually seen a few carrying long dead iphones."

"What do you mean by clones?" I asked out loud.

Josh answered me. "It may be a conspiracy theory, it may not be. C. theories have replaced the news these days, but this new breed almost has the wits of a man especially when fighting. However, when they're just stumbling around they're as dumb as squirrel turds."

"As far as conspiracy theories go--?" I started to ask.

"Save those questions for the boss. We have to get going," Josh ordered nervously looking around. Even with assault weapons, they had no wish to entangle with a horde of these ax wielding bastards.

They led us another hundred yards to some souped up looking van. It was what I considered a monster truck as it sat about four feet above the ground on some pretty big wheels, but when I told them that I thought it was a monster truck, they laughed at me. However it really did look like they were trying to get the Mad Max look. There were bars on the windows, gun ports, spikes that looked like horns on the front and back for ramming, and imposing armor plating. I understood the effect. Back in DC, I would have laughed at it for being cheesy because all that defense would be rendered useless by a stern look and a citation from a police officer. Here on the other hand, where I had witnessed just how cheap life is in my short stay, it was utterly terrifying. I could see the driver happily running over some poor schmuck without any legal ramifications.

The vehicle looked new or at least well maintained. However the front was dented in places and some of the spikes were bent. I didn't bother to ask what happened, because I wasn't sure if I would get a straight answer. Also I wasn't sure if I really wanted to know what caused the dents and I didn't need a good imagination to guess.

They loaded Bryan and Critter in first and then I climbed in and took a seat on the bench that lined the insides of the van. I purposefully sat across from Bryan and Critter for fear that they would kick my ass if I sat next to them. However, sitting across from them, I regretted having to feel their glares. Even when I avoided eye contact, I could sense their hatred. They really believed that I worked for The Specter. I thought we were getting along fine, but somehow I missed their suspicions lying just beneath their friendly smiles.

When all the soldiers found their seats, I burst out laughing when they took their uniform hats off. Josh had a regular military crew cut, but the rest of them had Mohawk haircuts. They were scary looking dudes, but it was the shock factor that caused me to laugh.

"What's so funny?" asked Josh.

"I'm not laughing at you. It was more of the shock value." I hesitated to mention the Mohawks. When I saw that he looked more curious than threatening, I told him, "The Mohawks. They just surprised me. It's like a standard post apocalypse movie from the 1980s."

Josh laughed and so did I. The other men then roared with laughter as well. I guessed within the safety of the truck they felt like they could finally relax.

Josh explained. "Hey, if that's who survives in the movies, we figured it might work in real life."

I nodded my agreement and said, "It looks like it is working."

"Yep. We're still above the dirt," said one of the crew.

The only people not laughing were the two prisoners.

"So far," Critter said with a grimness that hinted of a threat.

I furthered the joke, "Aren't all the Mohawk men in the movies the bad guys?'

The laughter suddenly died.

Josh thrust a hand at me with all four fingers and thumb pointed at my face. I thought he was about to kill me, and I don't say that lightly in this world. He screamed, "We are not the bad guys."

"OK, OK, man. I was just joking. Sorry."

"We don't joke! Never!" He screamed even louder. His face was red and looked about to explode.

The sound of the big diesel engine growled without any audio competition for a few moments. Slowly Josh cracked a grin. Immediately, everyone burst out laughing. I nervously joined in. Josh jovially slapped me on the shoulder a little harder than necessary.

"I'm kidding. You need to relax," said Josh.

"Yeah, Bryan keeps telling me that," I said, fully relieved. They had me for a moment.

A few others slapped me as well, giving full belly laughs.

"We'll get you a Mohawk if you want, when you join us." the ex cop said. I didn't know if he was serious or not.

I caught Critter's and Bryan's glare, but before I could react, the driver screamed a loud rebel yell that startled me even over the raucous laughter. "Time to lube the engine, boys! Hold on to your seats."

I suffered another startle as the van impacted something and a grey, red smear splattered on the windshield. The Low Boys cheered. Ahead, I saw a horde of about ten zombies. The driver purposely wove through, trying to hit all of them to the cheers of the men. A bit of the zombie stench found its way into the cab through the vents.

Unable to hold on, the prisoners were slammed to the metal floor from the combined impacts and sharp, sudden turns of the steering wheel. Both glared at me as if blaming me for the fall. I had a feeling that Bryan and Critter had a full tally of everything they blamed on my apparent betrayal.

The last zombie that the driver hit caused the engine to grind in a whiny, high pitched squeal.

Josh cursed, "That must be the cooling fan."

The driver yelled over his shoulder, "Hey, that wasn't my fault. You guys are my witness! I tried to drive around those freaks, but they jumped right in front of us. Eh?"

"There was a round of denials as to not having witnessed anything. I even gave my own denial to fit in. They laughed. "Even the new guy is with us," Josh chortled.

Josh looked at Bryan and Critter, "So, did you guys see that?"

Critter shook his head and shrugged.

Bryan said, "See what? I was knocked unconscious, jack-ass." It sounded rough, but it was said with the banter of two men who had been friends since childhood.

Josh nodded at Critter and Bryan. "I always liked you guys. I hope Craig goes easy on Y'all. I really do."

Bryan nodded back.

"I'll put in a good word for you, I promise," Josh added.

"Thanks," Critter said with a degree of respect.

Other than the whine of the damaged vehicle, we rode the rest of the way in silence. I stared out the window at the bleak winter landscape. The trees were as devoid of leaves as the road was devoid of people and cars. We did see an occasional abandoned vehicle, but nothing that was driveable. Occasionally, we'd have to drive around a car that was deserted in the middle of the road, but other than that it was an uneventful ride.

We drove through an abandoned small town. Vehicles and buildings with smashed windows greeted us. It was only slightly worse than Washington DC which had been spared the zombie apocalypse. That was it, other than four zombies that the driver took care to avoid hitting with the already damaged vehicle.

We drove through a deserted neighborhood, turned a corner, and I saw a huge rickety barrier that was a mix of a wall and fence. It stood about twelve feet tall and was constructed of everything from junked cars, barbed wire, tree trunks with burned pointed ends like you'd see protecting forts on old cowboy and western movies or anything else they could scrounge up to halt an enemy's advance. Occasionally, I would see a body of a zombie stuck with about a dozen arrows along the wall. Sporadically, there were watch towers posted along the barrier but not at equal distances. Although the distancing looked shoddy, I guessed that the placement was due to the effectiveness of observing the lines of fire due to obstruction from natural terrain or man made buildings.

Male and female guards along the posts were armed with both bows and arrows and rifles. I figured that the bow and arrows must have been for single zombies, whereas the rifles must have been in reserve in case of a full onslaught from a horde. A few dead zombies lay beneath the guard towers, feathered with many arrows. I guessed that the target practice was a pass time to deal with the drudgery of the duty as much as it was for protection.

We stopped at a gate that was once a sliding door for one of those huge old barns. It still had a coat of flakey red paint with white cross beams and frame. The men at the gate greeted us with a wave. One guard walked up to speak to us. The driver gave the guard a salute with the middle finger touching his forehead. The guard laughed and returned it.

Josh opened the rear sliding door on the van, and the guard acquired a more serious countenance and saluted with all five fingers. "Welcome back, sir."

"Thanks. Radio the boss and tell him that we succeeded more than anticipated," Josh ordered.

The guard looked at me and smiled like I was a celebrity. Then he looked serious as he digested Josh's command. He asked, "Should I tell him how much more than anticipated, sir? You know that the commander doesn't like surprises."

"He will this time," Josh said as he smiled at Critter and Bryan.

"Aye aye sir!" The guard said, but I could tell he was scared of making the call to the boss.

The guard pulled a rope and the gate gradually opened. When we drove past the gate I saw the man yell, "gate closing." He pulled a lever and the gate slammed shut as if it was propelled by large springs. I saw Critter and Bryan give each other a look that may have been shared worry. They had a manner of communicating without words. I swear they could speak paragraphs between each other without opening their mouths.

We stopped at an old mansion that seemed to serve as a headquarters. It was a historic southern gothic style building. I guessed that it followed a transition from a rich person's home, to a government building, to a tourist attraction. A two meter high granite monument on the front lawn confirmed that suspicion with a brief history etched into the stone. Unfortunately, I didn't get to read the history of the building, but nowadays it was obviously the headquarters for the town's paramilitary operations.

"Alright, out." Josh ordered gruffly. He seemed grumpier once in town.

I climbed out and offered to help Critter down the long drop from the raised frame of the van. He glared at me and then jumped, landing agilely despite his hands being bound behind his back. Bryan did the same. They both marched tall with their heads up and avoided looking at me.

As we walked to the building, I looked away from Bryan and Critter and enjoyed the sight of the towering mountains that ringed the town. As I did, I felt a shift in my thoughts as well as my literal vision as I looked over the new town. Those two didn't trust me. They thought that I had betrayed them and there was nothing I could say to change their minds. There was no action that I could take, either, to convince them of my innocence. Maybe this place was where I should be. My loyalty should ultimately be to me, not to those who want to kill me. I felt that there was no way I could regain Bryan and Critter's trust. So why bother? Should I give this place and these people a chance? I really didn't know, but as Bryan had said, I needed to be less inflexible.

| 8 |

As I was thinking that this town may become my permanent home, I was further inspired by the smell of fresh brewed and more importantly, fresh ground coffee beans. There is a smell that freshly ground coffee beans have that surpasses even the taste. The promise and the mental glorification of anything usually surpasses the real thing. I'm sure in heaven that the coffee will taste as good as it smells freshly ground.

A guard at the door stepped aside, saluted Josh, and said, "He's waiting for you, sir."

"Thank you, Private," Josh said as he returned the salute. I noticed they seemed to follow more of a protocol with rank and status once we were back in town.

The crew that had accompanied Josh now seemed on edge. The ex-cop said, "Sir, should we go back to the office?" This was the first time anyone in the crew had addressed Josh as sir. It seemed the soldiers had two different bearings, one for headquarters and one for anywhere else. In fact, the ex-cop seemed to wish to be anywhere other than headquarters. He bravely faced potential killers on the road with calm, yet he seemed apprehensive at seeing the town's boss.

"Yeah, I got this, Corporal." Josh said. "You're dismissed."

"Thank you, sir!"

After a sharp salute, the ex-cop rushed away at a quick walk. Josh motioned for me to enter the building ahead of the group. Aside from the banter in the van, he had avoided eye contact after mentioning his connection with Tommy. It was tempting to study his face for hints of what he was thinking. It would clue me in on how to act and when. For the present, I thought the best idea was to stay quiet, listen, and observe.

We entered the mansion and were led by two guards down a hall to a grand room. I hated the word grand in most cases, but from the chandeliers to the imprinted gold tin roof to the intricately hand carved wooden trim to even the immense size which was almost the size of a basketball gymnasium, it had all the grandeur of 1800s splendor.

My vision went to the big man with the shaved head forty yards across the room. He had a stance of supreme confidence. His feet were placed far apart and supported thick legs. His fists clenched at his waist with his elbows pointing out like wings. With his chin pointing slightly above our heads, he stood in front of a giant, intricately carved wooden chair that was almost more of a throne.

I did a double take. This was definitely the man I had seen in the drone footage while I was back in DC with Tommy. No doubt this was the guy who tried to jump Bryan and his family and then joined forces with them when the zombies attacked. It was a surreal moment for me.

The big man glared at us as we stood before him. It was an intense moment that ended when his stern face broke into a radiant smile and he spread his arms wide as if to offer a hug from forty yards, "Bryan, Bryan, Bryan!" His voice boomed brightly as if he was reunited with a long lost brother. "It's so good that you dropped by."

"Thanks for the escort, Craig," Bryan said dryly as Craig walked towards him with his muscular arms still outstretched. "Now if you'll untie me, I can return the hug."

Craig laughed. "You know I can't do that. And Critter! It is good to see you too, my man!"

Critter just nodded. A wry smile spread across his face as I saw his muscles tense against the ropes that bound his hands.

"Bryan," Craig said, shaking his head. " You're responsible for the death of three of my men."

I knew that Craig was referring to the video that I had witnessed, where Bryan had disabled two of them and the zombies ate them and a third man. However the four of them ganged up against Bryan.

It seemed like a few decades ago when I watched that video but it was only a week.

"The zombies got them," Bryan said with no emotion.

"After you slit one's throat and broke another's knee. What was in the backpack?"

"Cut the crap! Just untie us." Critter spoke up.

"Not yet!" Craig screamed as the smile immediately disappeared from his face. He suddenly seemed on the verge of exploding as he pointed his hand in Critter's face. "You will not give orders in my castle!" He shouted inches from Critter's impassive face. Craig's temperament resembled a time bomb with an erratic timer.

Craig then smiled jovially as if he hadn't just blown his top. The mercurial commander then said in a friendly tone, "We have some offers to make to your group, but we'll negotiate later. For the time being you can relax in a special room we have for you in the cellar."

Craig looked at Josh, "Did you search them, Captain?"

Josh answered, "Corporal Farnin did a quick search. We wound up just confiscating Critter's jacket. He had more knives in that than there are in cutlery store."

It may have been true. Critter had knives and throwing spikes hidden all over his body that acted as both weapons and protective armor as well.

Craig laughed. "Avoiding responsibility and placing it on your Corporal." Craig's face changed back to anger like a summer storm appearing suddenly over a ridgeline. "I asked if you searched them."

"I trust my men, sir," Josh replied.

"I haven't touched Critter, but I can see he's armed, Captain." He slapped Critter's shoulder and then felt around that area and laughed as he removed a small throwing spike from a hidden sheath in his long sleeve shirt.

"Strip them and search them for weapons and zombie bites." Craig said gently. As people just stared at him for the merest of moments, he exploded, "Now!"

"Yes, sir." Josh snapped his fingers and three men pointed their rifles at Bryan and Critter. Two other men untied the bonds. "Strip. Everything."

Bryan and Critter complied. Again their hateful stares were directed at me. The search that the guards performed was humiliating, but the glares should have been at Craig not me.

Another guard ruffled through their clothes and found two more knives. Naked, Critter and Bryan were tied up again.

"Your friends hate you." Craig said to me.

I was startled. Prior to this moment, Craig had treated me like I didn't exist. Now suddenly I felt like I was under his microscope. At this moment, I reasoned that there was nothing I could do to get back on Bryan's and Critter's good side, if I had ever been there. The stupid thing to do was to piss off Craig by attempting to fix the unfixable.

"They're obviously not my friends, the way they are acting. I stay loyal only to those who are loyal to me, and they are not loyal."

"Screw off—" Critter's growl was cut off by Craig's back hand across his face.

"Wise outlook," Craig said to me. Other than the backhand, Craig seemed to ignore Critter's anger. With a granite visage, Craig said to me, "You've caused us a bit of trouble, but that can be forgiven."

"How did I cause you trouble? I've been in the dark about everything since I embarked on this insane trip." I protested.

"We'll talk about that later," Craig said. He looked at the two captives. "Get them dressed."

The guards untied them quickly.

Bryan and Critter started to put on their clothes.

"No!" Craig's voice boomed. "They can still weaponize their clothes. I don't trust their ingenuity."

Some guards ran out of the grand hall and came back inside with some orange jumpsuits. Bryan and Critter put them on.

"Good, good," said Craig. "And as a reward for your coop-eration, give Eric Hildebrande back his weapons." He directed towards me.

I felt relief at this order. In my short visit to the Forbidden Zone, I had come to feel naked without my weapons.

"Not yet." A deep growl that sounded like a reverbed de-monic voice from a horror movie rumbled through the great hall. What was most intimidating about the deepness of the voice was that it sounded natural, not electronic or enhanced in any way.

Everyone turned to look where the voice had come from.

My blood went cold. The hooded and cloaked figure in black appeared from behind Craig's throne. He was mon-strous in size. The muscles rippled beneath his black tactical clothes as he walked toward us. The skull mask covered the features of his face. His eyes were dark in the recess of his hood. I couldn't tell if it was black paint around them or if it was his natural feature, but it made the whites of his eyes stand out like a candle lighting a skeleton's eyes. He was loaded with weapons. What caught my attention the most was a fantastical sword and a black assault rifle with a high-tech scope.

"Specter," Craig said in a fearful voice. "I didn't know you had arrived yet."

"You weren't supposed to," the rumbling growl emitted from inside the mask.

His eyes left Craig and focused solely on me. I was terrified.

"You," he simply growled.

He slowly walked towards me. I had seen him leap like a mountain lion upon a boulder that was at his head's level. I knew the explosive speed and power that the man-creature was capable of achieving. Somehow his purposeful slowness made him all the more terrifying. He covered the short distance in a time span that seemed more like minutes when it was really ten seconds at the most.

"You," he growled again. He made it to me and smacked me across the face with a back hand so hard that I hit the ground. I was too stunned to do anything. He began to kick me. The pain was intense, but I could tell the force he used wasn't to kill or injure but just to subdue me like a cruel owner will do to an animal, and I realized I was no more to him than a dog.

"You caused me much trouble, human," he growled.

"I—" I stammered.

"Take them all away," ordered The Specter. "I will deal with all of them later."

"Yes sir," said Craig. He then ordered his men with an urgent voice, "Take them to their accommodations."

The guards seized us to take to the dungeon.

| 9 |

Bryan, Critter and I were taken away and led down a great hallway. Three guards led us toward our cells, while three others followed with guns pointed at our backs. We then went down a flight of stairs.

Descending the stairs was like entering a completely different world. Where the first floor was lively and grand, the basement was dank and smelled like a tomb, a vampire's den. The rough unfinished stone and concrete walls were wet to the touch. Critter sneezed and blamed it on a mold allergy.

I did a double take. A single electric bulb at the bottom of the stairs poorly lit the entire basement. I wasn't sure if the power was from a generator, solar, or from a common source, but it was odd, the warm feeling I felt at just the sight of an electric light in the otherwise dismal basement.

I saw there were two cells and was happy they placed me into my own cell and kept Bryan and Critter together. Although they were tied up, I still remembered the ease in which they destroyed those two armed zombies with both hands tied behind their backs.

The cells were bare of any furnishing other than a cold stone floor. The bars looked like they had been fences for holding cattle in a pen. They were chained together and welded to steel posts that were embedded into the bedrock foundation. It was pretty sloppy but effective. The same bars that imprisoned me also protected me from Critter and Bryan.

The guards locked us in and left. One stayed behind to keep an eye on us. He looked around nervously and then pulled out a cellphone from a pocket in his uniform shirt. "Keep quiet and I will be cool. Narc on me and..." he let it hang as he started playing a video game.

"You got it bro," said Critter.

"Do you have a solar charger?" I asked the guard.

He gazed at me briefly then went back to his game, and mumbled, "Shut up. I ain't paid to talk to you."

The guard took a seat in the only chair in the entire basement and focused entirely on his video game. He was about twenty yards away. Far enough that Bryan, Critter, and I could converse without being overheard, especially as engrossed in the game and with the sound effects of the computer chirps and blips to drown out our whispers.

"Aren't we going to try to escape?" I asked. I was perplexed that they sat there and didn't struggle with their bonds or push their shoulders against the bars to test the strength.

"'We'll try to escape when you are not around," said Bryan.

"'Not your friends anymore,' huh?" Critter huffed as he quoted my words to Craig.

I had had enough of this crap. I stood holding the bars that separated us in a challenging manner as I said firmly, "Dude! You guys are treating me like crap. I didn't betray you, but you both stood there glaring at me like you wanted to kill me. What would you do in my situation?"

The guard looked up from his video game and glared at us until we all lowered our voices.

"How did you get that sword, from the vampires?" Bryan asked.

I sighed and actually told them the truth, at least everything that I knew. Maybe it was too strange to make up. Every time they asked me why, I could only shrug. Sometimes they asked me the same question multiple times. I wasn't sure if it was due to them trying to figure out what was up or if they were trying to trip me up and catch me in a contradiction. They listened and it was so weird they actually seemed to believe me, to a point.

When questioned about how The Specter knew where I would be and what he wanted, I responded that I knew less about that creep than anyone else.

"He beat the crap out of me and I never met him until last night, and he kicked my ass then too like he held a grudge against me. It's like he already knows me on some level."

"Why would someone want to kick your ass if they truly knew you?" Critter sarcastically quipped.

"So how did you kill the vampire chick, Abigail?" Bryan asked.

"I didn't. The Specter did it. But I think he just knocked her out. She was the same one who gave me the sword today." I explained. I then added the words, "I think," because I wasn't sure about anything.

"Why didn't you let me kill her last night?" asked Critter.

"I think she saved my life. I don't know why she did. She could have killed me easily either last night or earlier today. I felt like I owed her. Besides, I really did think that The Specter killed her when he laid her out. He hit her so hard that I thought her skull shattered or neck snapped. He scares the crap out of me. I didn't want you to mutilate what I thought was her dead body because, well, you're supposed to respect the dead."

"It's different when the dead don't stay that way," Critter replied with his usual calm but I could still sense a hint of superstitious dread in his voice.

"I wonder what the Specter has on Craig," Bryan said. "I've known Craig for years and have never seen him that worried and whipped. He's acting a little crazy."

"If the Specter enters their headquarters at will, I can see them having some kind of truce, but The Specter acts like he owns this place." Critter said as if trying to figure things out. "If Craig was all there, there's no way he'd let this happen. He's one of the toughest and most honest men I know."

"Is The Specter something supernatural?" I asked hesitantly. A day ago, I would have mocked anyone who asked such a question about any being other than zombies, but my outlook on life and reality had changed drastically in that short time.

"He's super something, but I don't think a ghost would need a night vision scope on his military issued rifle," Critter said with his wry smile.

"Then why doesn't someone kill him, I mean even a sniper shot from afar?" I asked.

"He's from beyond," said Bryan.

"From the Beyond?" I asked. I can only imagine how bug-eyed I must have looked, but it was enough to make Bryan chuckle and even the morose Critter half grin.

"No, no, no," Bryan rolled his eyes and explained, "From beyond the fence. Outside the quarantined zone. He either rides in the Blackhawks or he can call them in. He's rumored to have completely leveled a town. Only a handful escaped. Tomas was one of them. He could fill you in on more. As a reporter, it should be a good story. That atrocity needs to be reported-- unless you wind up working for The Specter."

"Never! By the way, I can only interview Tomas if you let me back into the tribe," I said.

Their faces seemed to turn to stone for a moment. They had gotten caught up in the conversation and forgot that I was considered their enemy.

I said, "Guys, I'm not your enemy. I'm probably even more confused than you."

"Yeah, whatever man," said Bryan. He turned and looked away. Critter had looked bored of the conversation before it had started, so I let go of the bars and just went to the corner of my cell, farthest from them and sat down.

I didn't wait long.

Craig ran down the stairs in a bit of a panic. He didn't even attempt to put on a warlord facade. The cacophony that he made on the ancient wooden stairs gave our guard plenty of time to hide his video game.

The guard stood ramrod straight and gave a hasty salute. Craig didn't return it. He waved a dismissive hand and said, "Guard, go upstairs until I call you."

"Aye aye, sir," said the guard.

As the guard ran up the stairs, Craig called him back.

"Yes sir," he exclaimed in a panicked state and tripped down a few steps before catching himself.

"I need the keys to the cells," Craig demanded.

The guard stumbled up to the commander and handed them over with a clank. Then the guard stood next to Craig.

"Go! Get lost!" Craig screamed with spittle flying from his command as he pointed up the stairs.

"Yes, sir!" Again, the guard shot up the stairs.

I scooted to the back of the cell as Craig came closer. There was something about his eyes as he approached with the keys to my cell. I couldn't read him, but there was an intensity about him that scared me. I backed into the corner and cringed as I heard the keys slide with a clinking sound into the lock. The door creaked open. I waited for him to draw his sword or gun to kill me.

Instead, he flung the door open wide and offered his hasty apology, "I am so sorry for the way you were treated. I have orders from up top to treat you well. However, I also have to obey The Specter. Usually they're on the same page, but The Specter doesn't like you."

Craig's apology was offered with a sense of fear. Looking back, I should have kept him worrying and not accepted it. However, I was too confused and scared myself to be able to figure out a coherent scheme, but I should have made the commander sweat.

"That's OK," I stammered.

"Good. Good, "he said quickly. "The Specter..." Craig couldn't seem to finish. It hung there and then the dungeon was silent.

I caught Bryan and Critter's facial expressions in a side glance. They looked equally perplexed.

"Where is The Specter?" I asked.

"He had to leave. He'll return later this evening. He wasn't supposed to be here this morning. You, Eric, are supposed to be turned into a vampire. Or maybe not. It's an honor and a curse." Each of his statements were blurted out in a staccato, with a panicked pause between each phrase that made the pronouncements seem like the random unrelated thoughts of a madman. I believed that Bryan's opinion that the master of Craigsville was indeed mad might just be correct.

This was when I forced myself to square my shoulders and faced Craig. In retrospect, I should have taken more interest in the threat of me being turned to vampirism, but my main goal was to take control of the conversation and make the leader make some sense. "What's this about The Specter? Do you run this place or not! You're obviously a powerful warlord and yet you simper in front of him. How can you command the respect of your men?"

I worried for a moment that I had gone too far, but Craig nervously looked over his shoulder, then at Bryan and Critter, then at me. "The Specter hates you."

"No kidding," I said, "but then why am I still alive?"

"I told you. Someone who controls him likes you." Craig then repeated. "The Specter hates you with a passion. I don't know what you did to him."

"I only just met him last night and he seemed to already have a grudge against me. If he's so powerful, why are you apologizing to me?"

I saw him sweating and shaking. I almost thought he might be having detox tremors. Craig blurted, "But his boss. You are special. His boss wants you well taken care of ..."

"What about me is so special? And who the hell is his boss? Tommy? The Governor?" I was getting frustrated. I felt there was something protecting me that went beyond my friendship with Tommy or even my uncle Daniel Hildebrande, who was the Governor of this FEMA Zone.

Craig's eyes enlarged as he considered where the orders came from.

"It's your DNA," he said. After a pause where he frantically looked around the room, he added, "I think. Your lineage." Craig giggled insanely for a brief moment.

"What do you mean by DNA and lineage? Are you talking about my uncle, the governor?"

Again his eyes widened. My uncle, the Governor, had supreme power over both the safe and the quarantined areas.

Craig said, "Maybe them. Maybe vampires. Maybe it's your destiny."

Bryan stormed up to the bars. His face was inches from Craig's. "What the hell is the matter with you Craig? Can I help you? Seriously, you need to get your balls back. You're acting like a scared little child. What happened to the man I knew? Despite all this, I'm still your friend. Let me help you."
Craig tried to interrupt a few times but Bryan kept talking as if trying to get through the fog that clouded Craig's judgement.

"Go to hell!" Craig finally screamed at him. "You don't know anything!"

Bryan shot back without flinching, "I know I don't know anything, so tell me so I can help you. I didn't say any of that to put you down. I said that with regards to our past friend-ship. Our children played together before all this went down. You suggested your youngest daughter marry my oldest boy. What happened to you?"

Craig looked at Bryan. His eyes windows to the gears of his brain churning along.

Bryan continued, "If your men see you as weak in the face of The Specter, a rebellion would surely follow. I know how groupthink works and the stress that you carry on your shoul-ders, brother."

Craig nodded aware that he was receiving sage advice. "Bryan, you don't even know the half of it! Hell, I don't. If you knew what I knew, you would ask me for your weapons back so you could put a bullet through your own head."

Bryan opened his mouth to shoot something back, but instead the two men held eye contact. Almost as if testing and reading the strength of each other's inner steel.

The fire burning in Bryan's eyes diminished and he nodded. "I see. Be careful, my friend."

"Thank you," said Craig. "I'll see what I can do for you as well, but you're not held under my orders. I don't want my town leveled and people killed by The Specter's helicopters."

"Why does he want us?" Bryan asked.

"I am not sure," said Craig, but I will do my best for you. I promise."

"Thanks," Bryan said. "As a sign of good faith, could you at least untie us?"

Craig seemed to regain his composure. He was again the warlord. "You know that I can't do that. You would laugh at my request for the same if the situation was reversed."

Bryan looked Craig straight in the eyes and replied, "If the situation was reversed I would remember our past friendship despite the desires of a spooky character in a Halloween mask and black hooded cloak. I would not fear you because you were my friend and I value such things." Bryan went back to sitting on the floor in his corner of the cell.

Critter's eyes were off in the distance and I assumed his mind wandered some forest beyond the rock walls of the basement.

Craig ignored Bryan's taunt and turned to me and said, "Come on, Eric. I have things to show you."

| 10 |

I nervously followed Craig up the stairs and blinked in the sunlight when the door opened at the top. Once we were back into the opulence of the mansion, Craig was in full control again.

Craig addressed the guard, "Go back down there and keep a sharp eye on the prisoners," he said in a deep commanding voice.

As the guard turned to go, Craig placed a firm hand on his chest stopping him. Craig reached in the guard's chest pocket and pulled out the cellphone. Craig held it in one hand as he said, "and don't let me catch you playing with yourself again or having this thing glued to you face." Craig punched the screen leaving a cracked indentation in the glass in the shape of three of his knuckles. He handed the shattered phone back to the guard.

The guard received it with a, "Yes sir," and hurried down the stairs.

Craig turned and addressed me pleasantly, "Come with me. I'll show you your new home."

We exited the mansion and walked down the main road through the small town. The temperature had climbed to a comfortable 60ish degrees and the radiant sun felt warm on my face. It was one of those glorious winter days when everything thaws and you can smell the wet dirt and the green sprouts reaching from the earth towards the sun. The promise of spring.

There was another smell that took a moment to register. I thought the roads in this town were full of dirt until I saw a horse go by pulling a wagon. Then it struck me. The dirt in the streets was horse crap. It struck me as odd, my reaction to the scent. Horse manure had a homely smell, maybe it was from some past life or an experience encoded in the DNA, but the faint smell was actually pleasant. Although I realized it was probably due to the cold weather dampening the smell. I could only imagine how nasty it would be in the summer with flies carrying it around. This made me wonder if the stench of dead zombies was becoming unbearable at the Mountain Warrior camp with the warmer temperatures.

"Paradise, ain't it?" Craig said with a humorous tone. He emphasized the word ain't as if to tell me, I can speak proper English, but I will say ain't to offend your North Eastern sensibilities.

I looked around the valley almost as if for the first time. When I first arrived, my focus was on my immediate circumstances and whether I would survive. Arriving here as a prisoner, I mostly kept my eyes on my captors to be on guard if they would strike me or shoot me. Also, in any one hour that I had spent in the Forbidden Zone, I had seen more guns than I had seen in my entire life and that narrowed my peripheral vision tremendously. To see that much firepower wielded by people I didn't trust was unsettling. I was determined that when given a chance, I would get a gun and never relinquish it. I had had enough of being at the mercy of others.

In the camp of the Mountain Warriors we were ensconced in a high mountain valley. Missing the mountains was like missing the forest for the trees. Living in the wilds, I was too concerned with surviving to appreciate the beauty.

Walking down the block in Washington DC you were aware that if you walked further down the street there were only more city blocks, as far as the eye could see. In Craigsville, as you looked down the street you saw mountains towering thousands of feet above the buildings just a few blocks away. It was like someone cut out a section of the city and replaced it with a postcard scene.

"This is really beautiful," I told Craig.

"You'll get used to it," he said with odd neutrality.

"So where are we going?" I asked.

"This is your new home. The Specter wants you to feel welcomed."

"Thanks," I said agreeably, knowing that The Specter didn't care about my comfort. "I would have really felt welcomed with that fresh ground coffee that I smelled back there." Even back home, it had been a year or so since I had that.

"Oh sorry. I should have offered. Things have been very crazy," he said with a light but wildish laugh.

He didn't see me nod, but I didn't bother to express anything out loud because he seemed preoccupied.

We arrived at a police station and entered. He reintroduced me to Josh. I shook Josh's hand as Craig introduced him as, "Captain Joshua Righter, my right hand man."

Josh nodded at me and looked back to Craig as if awaiting orders.

Craig gave them. "Introduce Eric Hildebrande around as I discussed earlier and get him back to the mansion just before nightfall." Craig immediately left without another word.

Josh watched Craig leave with a slightly perplexed look on his face. Then he leaned in and whispered after the door slammed behind Craig, "This stays between us. I'm telling you this because Tommy told me to work with you, but I'm worried about the boss. He used to rule with an iron fist. He was fair but very firm, but that Specter guy has taken over somehow. Not just Craig's town, but his soul. He looks weak in front of his people and no leader can afford that."

I nodded. The information worried me. This was not something to tell an outsider immediately. He didn't know where my loyalties lie. I wondered what all Tommy had told Josh and if something was afoot that would go down soon. The idea of a civil war happening in the town just as I arrived worried me, but whether he was a just good stoic or truly at peace with the crazy world, Josh didn't seem too out of sorts. So I tried to remember Bryan's advice to relax my tense shoulders and let them float on my ribcage rather than welding them to my neck. I lowered my shoulders and rocked my head back and forth hoping it would help.

We left the police headquarters. When walking with Craig, I noted that most people avoided eye contact with him out of fear. With Josh, I could tell he held the same respect of the town folks, but they didn't have fear of him. Josh also seemed to know everyone's name. Craig's leadership was that of an enforcer. Josh was more of a statesman who just happened to carry an assault rifle.

"Hey, Gerty," he addressed an older woman.

"Good afternoon, Captain Righter," she said and started to walk away.

"Just a moment, ma'am. This here is Eric Hildebrande," Josh introduced.

I shook her hand. It was cold with age, but her old eyes were warm with southern hospitality.

When she heard my last name, her thin eyebrows arched, "Oh. Like the governor."

"Yes ma'am. I am his nephew and adopted son," I said with slight embarrassment.

Josh nodded, "Eric is a great author and he is going to film a documentary and write a book about how we're surviving here in the Appalachian Mountains."

"Oh my, Like the Foxfire series. That is so exciting to have someone so famous among us," Gerty exclaimed.

"I'm not really that famous, and my journalism career hasn't been that stellar either, but I'll do my best," I said as I shifted my feet.

She looked disappointed.

"Well, we gotta be going," Josh said to her, "but don't let his false humility fool you."

"You take care Captain. And it was good to meet you, Mr. Hildebrande."

"You can call me Eric."

As she walked away Josh snatched me by the wrist. "Listen!" He said through gritted teeth like a Sergeant about to tear into a new recruit. He stopped and suddenly let go of my wrist. He held his hands up and patted the air as if his hands were apologizing for the affront. He sighed and said, "Listen," again in a more reasonable tone and then again even calmer as if trying to do a start over, "Listen. You're supposed to be some big shot. You're here to give people hope that the grind of modern life will lead to some form of immortality through your documentary."

"Is this what Commander Craig said?"

"The commander said it a little more crudely, but basically similar, yes. You are not to make disparaging remarks about yourself. Do you understand? Allow them to believe what they see, especially if they think you're bigger than you are. They need hope. You're to give that hope. Understood? This is important."

I nodded, more than his words, I could see in his eyes that he meant it.

"When you're addressed by a title, you accept it. Live it. That is the way of thing. Do you understand?"

"Yes, Captain Righter."

"By the way," he said. "You can call me Josh. You're in the top echelon with us. Welcome aboard," he said with a wry smile and an extended hand.

I shook it, "I hear you loud and clear, Josh."

He introduced me to more people in the next hour. I had a feeling that he was running for office in the way he spoke to even the lowliest citizen. He commanded respect, but he seemed to deeply care about the people. I came to this conclusion in the way his eyes delved into another person's soul and his tone of voice, not just his choice of words. He also didn't talk badly about people behind their backs like I had seen others in power do after pretending to be gracious to their face.

Soon, word spread and people came up and introduced themselves to me. They were even requesting autographs. I was everything from a TV producer, reporter, and author with political connections to the outside according to the wildfire that was the town's rumor mill. Not only was I famous, but anyone that attracted my attention could become the next star. As insane as it sounds, I was probably the first thing that resembled hope to come into their lives since it all went down.

A part of me relished in it. The Mountain Warriors saw me as a fool at best, but despite my instant status, something didn't feel right. It wasn't in the scheme of things but rather internal. I felt like I was being set up to disappoint everyone.

As I mulled this over, Josh told me that we had about an hour and a half until dark. He nervously looked at the sky and suggested that we go to the chow hall. My belly coincidentally growled in concurrence. He pointed the way and we walked about one hundred yards to an old style cafeteria diner. It had a log cabin facade, but I could tell that the logs were actually plastic. The interior was a large square room full of tables. From observing the line of cafeteria style serving trays, it was obviously food that was mass produced. Actually it looked like the cooking process involved opening economy cans of beef stew and vegetables and then simply warming it all up.

Granted, it wasn't that bad. I had read that some 80% of the population of the Forbidden Zone had died of starvation, attacks from both zombies and living people, lack of medicine and other inconveniences of a post apocalypse world in the last two years. To any survivor, canned food easily beat starvation.

However, Josh still saw me making a face and said, "That's not for you. From now on, you get to eat in the officer's mess."

"Does everyone eat this well here?"

He replied, "Just those who work. We've had a good store of food because there were very few survivors. We'll start to run low in the next few months and will have to make a raid on Asheville." Josh finished with a frown.

"Why did you make that face about Asheville?"

"That place is loaded with zombies." He chuckled as if at some great bitter irony.

"What's so funny?" I asked.

He snorted and said, "Nothing much has changed in Asheville since it all went down."

I still looked at him curiously. I had heard that Asheville was a pretty cool place, in the before.

His face displayed a combination of irritation, embarrassment, then he smiled genuinely. He had the look of someone forced to explain a badly delivered joke, "It's the redneck in me talking. Asheville was full of every type of zombie: hippies, hipsters, yuppies, you name it," he explained. Then he added, "Pardon me. One develops a dark sense of humor out here. Just don't lose your soul in the process. I knew plenty of great people who lived there. Lots of good people everywhere died," he added musingly.

I nodded and faked a laugh. In reality those were more my type of people. I was a city boy, but I was looking to fit into the place where I was stuck, so I hoped my laugh sounded genuine. I felt like I was being a phony, but this went beyond mere peer pressure and desire for group acceptance. This was for survival.

Josh led me to an area cordoned off by a divider curtain made of folded wooden slats used to section off rooms. Once inside and seated, a chef walked up to the table, after an exchange of greetings and introductions, the chef said, "You are in luck! Craig had just ordered one of our sacred cows to be slaughtered."

When Josh saw me raise an eyebrow, he laughed, "We call them sacred because they are scarce and well guarded. Indeed, this is a treat. Canned food and wild game gets old day after day." Josh looked to the cook and asked with some excitement, "So what does that get us? One of your legendary hamburgers?"

The chef actually frowned and replied with a spark of humor, "You insult me. For our Captain of the guard and our town's new and only celebrity, we have porterhouse steaks."

"Oh, Chef Randy you are a God among men and nothing less!" Josh exclaimed.

"How do you want it? Medium? Well?"

Josh interrupted the Chef, "Bloody as hell, as Steve Buscemi would put it."

"Very good. From Pulp Fiction," said the chef. "And you?"

There were vegetarian options, but since I was getting a degree of respect so far, I really didn't want a repeat of when Scott had made fun of me and made a crude remark about my sexual preferences based on my dietary decision, "I will take bloody as hell for 1000, Alex."

"Great choices. I'll sear them and be right back as soon as the steaks cry, 'moo,'" he said. "The steaks will be served with fresh mashed potatoes topped with beef gravy, but unfortunately the green beans are canned."

"Awesome," said Josh. "No apology is needed chef."

"Yes. Thank you," I said with true gratitude.

The chef bowed graciously and left on his mission.

Josh leaned back in his chair looking distantly past the ceiling, I could tell that a pressing weight sat on his mind. He blew out a burst of air and looked at me. "We need to talk," he said as if everything between us was lies.

"I am all ears."

"What's your opinion on all this?"

"All this what?" I asked.

"Don't play coy," he said angrily.

I was understandably taken aback. I replied, "I really don't know where to start. I was banished from the Safe Zone to the Forbidden Zone two days ago. Before that I had never held a real weapon besides a butcher's knife. I had some sword training but never had to apply it in real life. Last night, I had to kill hundreds of zombies using both sword and firearm, or I would not be alive right now. "

"You took down those two maniac zombies like you knew what you were doing."

"I guess I had good teachers," I said trying to put in a good word for my friends. "Those, Mountain Warriors as some call them, are good people"

"That's what I was going to ask you about. What's the word?"

I looked at him curiously. He was holding something back. "Get to the point," I finally said.

He blew out a breath of air again and leaned forward, "What I'm going to say could get me sent to a firing squad or far worse. Far far worse than you can imagine." He glared at me until I nodded. I realized that what I was seeing in him wasn't anger, but sheer terror. He was a man of action who turned fear into anger and determination, and then into accomplishment. "I have some orders, from that mutual friend of ours, to get you out of town immediately. A faction of those in power want to turn you into a vampire. Another faction is against that-- those are the ones who want you out of here. However, we all need to fight this."

He paused so I prompted with an, "OK."

He continued, "Those are honest men and women living in the mountain, the Mountain Warriors as you call them. I mean, they would work for the betterment of mankind. I know them. They're good people. I think you're a good man, too. This is it, all good men and women need to work together against The Specter and who he works for."

I nodded in agreement. How could I disagree with a platitudinous statement.

Josh continued, "Craig is weak. He has sold us out for whatever reason. He-- He feeds our town folks to those vampire things. I sent some good men to their cave last night." He made a face like he couldn't finish a confession. After a pause he said, "I would rather catch a bullet than live with that on my conscience any longer. I want to form an alliance with the good men and women in our settlement and the Mountain People. I'm telling you all this because our time is short."

"What's The Specter's game?" I asked. "I don't trust him at all, but not knowing what he's up to makes it even worse."

Josh shook his head no and looked like he had something horrible in his mouth that he wanted to spit out. "It's probably better that you don't know. Those frickin vampires—" he couldn't finish.

"Are they real vampires? They worry me, but they also remind me of those wannabes who dress up freaking weird and hang out together and do, whatever." I played dumb. I knew they were real of course, but I didn't want to admit that I knew a few by name.

Josh nodded in agreement, "As with everything, I am not sure what's a show and what's for real and more importantly, what is being hidden, but they, the vampires, are real and all of them are evil incarnate."

I blurted out, "They seem to have some kind of mind control."

"Have you had contact with them?" He seemed to look right through me and focus on a point far behind my head.

I reluctantly nodded.

He looked fearful for a moment. "No one I know has talked to them and survived, other than Craig."

I told him, "I was alone in the woods when the vampires approached me. Some men from the Mountain Warrior tribe showed up and the vampires fled. I was under the spell of one of them, a woman. To be honest, I think she was trying to save me from the others."

He whistled, impressed. "You are a very lucky man. What did they do to you?"

"They drew their swords. It was weird. I felt like my mind was cloudy. I lost track of time."

"What do you mean lost track of time?"

"They were twenty feet from me when I closed my eyes. When I opened them, a vampiress was literally at my throat. It scared the crap out of me, but oddly, I wasn't worried until later when I could process it. Despite what they are, I think she may be an ally."

"Is she younger, long dark hair, fairly attractive?" he asked.

"Her name is Abigail, I believe."

He glared at me with the same suspicion that Critter and Bryan had.

I held up my hands and said, "I've already been searched for bites."

Josh nodded but still had a hard time digesting what I told him. It must have been unbelievable to these survivors. Maybe they just didn't want to believe it. These were tough guys who had experienced most kinds of combat here against zombies, many were veterans of foreign conflicts, but I imagine that mind control from the vampires must have been something that seemed not just deadly but off limits.

Josh began by whispering harshly through gritted teeth and then his voice raised with his emotion, "That's what pisses me off. The Specter is forcing Craig to make truces with every abomination to mankind. He won't make peace with survivors such as the Mountain folks-- our friends and neighbors, but he will with those blood suckers. It's an abomination in every Biblical sense of the word. Listen, I'm not being melodramatic with the word abomination. I know that you writers are like wordsmiths. They mean something, but I ain't hyperbolizing. There's some really awful things happening—"

"What?" I asked as he paused. His eyes were distant as if seeing some horror from the past. I pressed him, "What exactly is happening?"

"They-- Craig punishes people by stripping them and leaving them in the woods for the vampires. I actually order our men to drop the condemned off. It's part of our treaty with those blood suckers. I've heard their screams, even over the engines, as we drive away. Not just loud, but you can hear utter terror. I've been a soldier most of my adult life and have never heard cries like that. I can't imagine dying in such a manner."

"What manner?" I prompted.

"I find their bodies the next day. It's not just the wounds. It's the look on their face like a dead skin mask. I allowed them to send a childhood friend to the vampires once. No one told me where Douglas was going, but deep inside I know he's never coming back." He placed his head in his hands. Then he looked at me with raw determination. "That's why I am not pulling you out! We're fighting these things in the next few hours!"

I was about to ask what my part in fighting the vamps was, but we both jumped as Chef Randy returned with our plates.

After we said our thanks and Chef Randy returned to the kitchen, I asked Josh, "What kind of truce is Craig making with the vamps and how am I supposed to fight them?"

He shook his head. "We'll talk more after dinner. My food won't digest with my thoughts in disarray, but I must know, will you stand with us against the monsters of our time or will you sell your soul to them? We need a hard nose journalist to get this information out of our town and to the world. Where do you stand?"

"I am with the good guys," I said. I was honest in this statement. I planned to do what was right to the best of my ability, but I wasn't really sure who the good guys were. I definitely did not like The Specter. The vamps rightfully gave me the creeps, but I felt I had an odd alliance with Abigail. Craig was unstable. Josh seemed solid, but I hadn't known him that long and I didn't know what he was up to. Even with him in contact with Tommy, I was suspicious about him telling me so much information. The Mountain Warriors took me in and I appreciated them helping me, but I also took Critter at his word when he said that he would kill me. So yes, I would stand with the good guys, when I figured out exactly who they were. Until then, I was out for myself as selfish as that might sound.

Josh nodded, seemingly pleased with my answer. He bowed his head and his lips moved silently in prayer before eating. He looked up when he was done and smiled like we never had the earlier conversation. The prayer, and the placing his trust in something other than himself seemed to still his mind at least long enough to enjoy his steak, mashed potatoes and green beans, all slathered in gravy.

We both cut into our steaks. I watched the clear red juice leak out as I cut into it and took a bite. I chewed it and savored the flavors. This was the second time that I had eaten meat today and today was the first time in about a year. The steak almost melted in my mouth in contrast to the chewy venison. Chef Randy had seasoned it perfectly. The balance of salt, garlic, and char was delightful. However, the beef tasted tame. That is the best word I could give it. The venison had a vibrant, wild taste that I oddly preferred, but I withheld that critique.

"Are you a religious, spiritual man?" Josh asked me.

I swallowed the food in my mouth and replied, "I never would have considered myself to be before, but I've probably prayed more in the last couple days than I have in my entire life."

He laughed, "I can believe that. When you walk the line between life and death on a daily basis, you need to balance your thoughts so you're at peace with both life and death. The scary thing is that I feel more at peace with death than life at this point."

"You fear life more than death?"

He spoke as he chewed his beans, "I don't fear living, I fear what this life has become. I fear the dishonesty and inhumanity that we have devolved into. I suspect that the vamps and zombie abominations are the results of people screwing with nature to extend life and power beyond what nature intended. Rumor has it the zombie virus was code named 'Operation Fountain of Youth'."

I watched him as he ate robotically. He seemed to derive no pleasure from his steak. He left his peace place that the prayer had brought. A vision of a very dark future colored his eyes.

"So, it was a virus?" I asked.

"Hell, I don't know. The rumor mill has replaced our nightly news cast." He chewed some more meat and then looked at me. "You're with the good guys, eh? I'll be needing to talk to those Mountain folks and put things right."

"You can count on me," I said with full sincerity on my face. However, deep inside, I wondered if I was lying to him. With death all around, I didn't know if I had the courage to back up my convictions. I hoped that I would.

My mind however went back to Peter with the fractured leg and likely infection due to my accidental firing of the gun. If anyone was deserving of life, it was the man who bravely dealt with his wound back at the camp. "Is there a pharmacy in town?"

Josh nodded.

I said, "I need to get some antibiotics up to the Mountain Warrior's camp. Someone broke a leg."

He didn't seem too worried.

So I explained further, "You could see the bone fragments and muscles through the skin and there was lots of blood. Pus was starting to leak from the wound this morning. It smelled horrible."

I was going to describe more, but he waved the palm of his hand in the universal signal to stop. He then pointed to his plate as he chewed his meat. He swallowed and said, "OK. OK, I got it. It complicates things, but it may solidify an alliance between Craigsville-- I'm changing that name, Craigsville, as soon as I am in charge. I'm glad to see that you care for others. Most people would be thinking of just saving their own skins. I'll get some medicine up there somehow as a gesture of goodwill, but just in case anything happens to me,

I'll point you to the pharmacy. It's on our way back to head-quarters."

"What do you think may happen to you?" I asked.

He just shook his head and said, "It's some rough times. You can't take anything for granted. Craig is paranoid."

I had a ton of questions to ask, but at that moment the ex-cop who captured us arrived at the table and announced, "Sir. You are wanted at headquarters immediately."

"What's the matter Corporal?"

"I don't know Captain. I am just relaying orders, but it looks bad."

"Thanks. You may go," Josh replied with a worried look.

The ex-cop looked at the remains of our dinner and whistled. "That looks good. I gotta get promoted to officer ranks."

Josh replied, "Just wait until we succeed, Corporal. Now go eat and relax."

The Corporal/ex-cop regretfully shook his head no, "I'm supposed to go back immediately and tell them you're on the way, sir."

Josh nodded and dismissed him, "Very well, Corporal."

As the Corporal ran back to headquarters, I said to Josh, "You guys were quite casual in the field but very formal in town."

He replied, "We're a very tight knit group. Inside town, Craig has a set of formalities that we must follow. Outside, we're friends. Very few people in town brave going outside the walls. There's a brotherhood among us whose duty it is to hunt, scrounge, or defend. You probably understand with the short time you've been in the mountain camp."

I cocked my head not quite sure what he meant.

He continued, "Either the Mountain Warriors think very highly of you, enough to let you accompany them on their missions," he said seriously, then he chuckled and said, "or they're trying to get rid of you like a dog left on the side of the road."

I nervously chuckled in reply.

"Let's go," Josh said as he wiped his lips with a napkin and stood up. "I'll show you where the pharmacy is."

We walked out of the officers area. The cafeteria was now packed with the lower ranking soldiers gratefully getting their scoop full of canned slop. Despite being a vegetarian (actually a former vegetarian,) I was grateful for the steak dinner over the beef stew.

***

Tommy watched Josh and Eric leave the chow hall on his computer screen. A lot flowed through his mind after listening in on the conversation that was recorded by the hidden microphones in the walls. Tommy was a bit surprised at Eric's street smarts. He answered very neutrally so as not to incriminate himself with either side, but rather to set Josh's mind at ease. However, Tommy wished he had a better clue as to what Eric was thinking.

Tommy blinked his eyes and rubbed his weary face as he looked away from the computer monitors. He leaned back in his expensive, ergonomically correct office chair that some-how was the least comfortable piece of furniture that he had ever owned. He tried to relax his mind, but he was getting wrapped up in the drama unfolding before his eyes.

Josh knew that a lot of places in Craigsville were bugged, and that idiot may have ruined everything or almost every-thing. Tommy guessed that Craig sending his buddy Douglas to die was too much. Josh may not have been in the loop, but he was a sharp man. Even without evidence, it was ob-vious that people were disappearing. Death was fairly com-mon and with +80% of the population dying in two years, soldiers getting killed on patrol wasn't too surprising. Besides, no one wanted to believe that their leader sent men to feed the vampires. Craig grew up in that small town. Everyone had known him since he was a kid.

Josh obviously had enough and would not hide. He was a warrior and ready to fight, but this rash action on his part made Tommy suspect that Josh was fusing out. The problem was that Josh was doomed to die, and because of his obstinate streak, Eric would get turned into a vampire.

Tommy swore. He was really concerned for Eric but couldn't figure a way out for him now that Josh had decided to fight rather than run. Yes, it was a bit of a double cross to get Eric into the Forbidden Zone. However, Eric needed the shove. Under pressure, his old friend could usually pull a sur-prise. He was thriving now as he lived with death instead of slowly drowning in degeneracy back home. However now the pressure was too much.

Tommy did want Eric to make a kick ass documentary. Yes, it would give Tommy a hit TV show, and yes, winning the heart of Jennifer, Eric's ex-girlfriend was all part of the plan, but there was no way in hell, he could let Eric get turned into the undead.

Tommy was sure that The Spector was well aware of the conversation between Josh and Eric already, so Tommy called him quickly.

He got the voicemail and left a brief message, "Hey it's Tommy. It looks like Josh is trying to ruin our plans. Call me."

Tommy had regrets about Josh, but The Spector already knew, so pretending to fill him in would only keep Tommy away from suspicion.

He sighed as he watched the screen. The only way his friend Eric could avoid the bite of the vampiress now, was up to his own resources. Tommy could only watch.

| 11 |

Josh and I left the chow hall and quickly walked down the street. I was soon able to see the mansion towering above the other houses like the mountains towered above the town. I knew that was our destination, but Josh led me down a side street.

"Where are we going?" I asked

"This is the shortcut to the pharmacy."

The side street connected to another main road and the pharmacy was one of those old fashion white painted wooden buildings instead of the faux-brick, glass, and plastic that were ubiquitous where I was from. Although it needed some repairs, it still looked sturdy. I tried to observe the building like Bryan or Critter would, checking out the potential ways in and out, in case we needed to quickly raid it on the escape from Craigsville.

The town had recently installed bars over the window to prevent break ins. It wasn't pretty, but it looked like the bars would effectively prevent a burglary. I thought that if we did raid it, the bars may wind up being a prison rather than defense if the town's guards surrounded us. I also noticed that the pharmacist who I saw through the window was armed with a rifle. He was an older man, but he looked like he was made of steel. The way he held himself, I got that feeling he was a Vietnam veteran or something. I saw his white coat and then something dawned on me.

I told my observation to Josh. "I've noticed that the only people in town who carry firearms are dressed in paramilitary uniforms. It seems that most civilians, other than the pharmacist, are pretty much unarmed. Most everyone in the Mountain Warrior camp, though, is fully armed."

"The mountain folks don't have the luxury of a zombie wall. So up there every able bodied citizen has to take responsibility and basically be their own bodyguard. Unfortunately, when someone who doesn't know what they're doing gets a gun, there's a chance of an accidental discharge, like yesterday. I heard that the zombie horde that attacked the Mountain Warrior camp was caused by a discharged firearm. Was that from an intruder or just some idiot?"

He looked at me as if hoping I could fill in some details on what came to him through the rumor mill.

Feeling embarrassed, I shook my head and said, "A bit of both, I guess. It was some dumbass kid." That statement was somewhat truthful. I had overheard Adam refer to me as "that dumbass kid," yesterday. I guessed old Adam considered anyone under fifty to be a kid.

"Could I go inside? I'd like to talk to the pharmacist." I said.

Josh instinctively looked at his wrist that held no watch, then at the rapidly setting sun, and grimaced. "OK, but hurry."

I nodded and said, "It'll be quick."

I ran for the door and realized that I startled the pharmacist who raised his rifle like a rattlesnake will raise its head. He didn't point it at me, but he let me know he was ready. I slowed my run and raised my empty palms to my chest. He responded by lowering the gun and gave me a questioning look as I opened the door. "Is there an emergency?" he asked.

I skipped all introduction and launched into the tale of Peter and his broken leg.

He nodded sagely. "We do have some clindamycin which will help with osteomyelitis, but he'll need more surgical care than what Adam or Bryan could give."

I cocked my head, "They are surgeons?"

"Adam technically is. He is a veterinarian."

He responded to me when I looked more inquisitive. "People are animals too, you know. Same anatomy and physiology, just a slightly different structure."

I nodded and asked, "Is Bryan a veterinarian too?"

"No, he was a chiropractor."

"Chiropractors do surgery?" I asked flabbergasted.

"They do now, especially if they're taught by a competent veterinarian," he said with a hint of irony under dark gray eyebrows thick as a summer storm cloud. "They don't tend to check licenses these days."

"Yeah, I guess the world has changed."

"To put it mildly," he said with a half grin.

I could see Josh shifting his weight slightly from one foot to another like a child who had to use the potty. I got back to the point, "Could I get that antibiotic, *Clinicyn?*" I asked and cringed as I realized that I had horribly mispronounced it.

Josh entered the pharmacy, nodded to the old pharmacist, and then just glared at me.

The pharmacist nodded back at Josh and answered me, "Clindamycin. Sorry. That can only be released by an order from Commander Craig Hobart. Even Captain Righter can't authorize that request"

Josh saw his queue, "Speaking of Commander Craig, we need to get to headquarters, right now."

The old pharmacist nodded in agreement and said, "The sooner you get there, the sooner you get permission."

I looked at Josh and said, "Let's go."

As we exited the building I saw Josh glance nervously at the direction that the sun had set. All that was left was a red line along the top of the western ridge as the residual light seeped out of the town. Josh took off at walking pace so fast that I had to jog a few steps on two occasions to keep up. Once we arrived back at headquarters, we were quickly led into what I called the grand throne room.

Commander Craig greeted us and walked straight to me from the throne. "Eric, Eric, welcome back. How did you enjoy the tour of your new home?"

The ex-cop stood guard next to the empty throne. I couldn't place my finger on it, but he looked tense or worried about something. At first, I guessed it was from standing guard at headquarters. He struck me more as a person who liked the action of the field rather than the formalities of town.

I answered Craig as I mulled the disposition of the ex-cop, "It's really nice, sir. I have yet to get 'used to' the splendor of the mountains as you put it."

Josh added, "He's met a lot of the town folks and they love him."

Craig completely ignored Josh and replied to me, "Yes, the scenery is striking and that's what gives character to the people who inhabit this region."

I noticed the ex-cop seemed to be trying to signal Josh by pressing his lips together and moving his eyes side to side.

I replied to Craig. "There is a definite grit to the people of this region. I read the Foxfire series when I was a kid."

"Really?" Craig giggled. "That's impressive, reading the whole series as a kid."

"Well, actually, my folks had them. I mostly looked through the pictures and occasionally read a chapter."

"Sounds about right," said Craig.

"But I did acquire a great degree of respect for the people of this region," I said worrying that I might be laying it on too thick.

Craig giggled again, this time it bordered on sounding crazy. He said, "Had the zombie plague hit Washington DC instead of the Appalachian area, there would have been no survivors."

I laughed and said, "To borrow Captain Righter's description of Asheville, I don't think the zombie like people in DC would have changed that much either."

I was expecting Craig to make that annoying high pitch giggle, but instead he turned livid at the mention of Captain Righter.

"Corporal!" Craig screamed.

"Yes, sir," answered the ex-cop.

"Place the Captain under arrest," the Commander ordered.

"Aye aye, sir," the ex-cop answered. He approached Josh and I saw him silently mouth, "Sorry," and began to tie Josh's hands behind his back. Josh gave no physical resistance.

"Commander. This is a mistake," Josh verbally contested.

"No! My sources told me that you're plotting to overthrow me and that you have a secret alliance with our enemies!" Craig accused angrily.

"What enemies? You know I don't trust the vampires," Josh said.

"He's secured, sir," the ex-cop replied in an officious tone.

Craig noticeably relaxed when Josh was tied and only then he stepped up to Josh's face and said, "Not them. The vampires are our friends."

"Who then?" Josh asked.

"The Mountain Posers," Craig giggled at his nickname for them. "Don't worry. I'll see that you get a fair trial. Corporal! Take him away!" Craig pointed and ordered with all of the melodrama you'd see in a movie. This position of power really hit him in the head quite hard.

Craig watched, with fist clenched and arms akimbo as the ex-cop led Josh away. He did a double take at me as if he forgot that I was standing there. After a moment of considering me, he said, "Follow me, Mr. Hildebrande."

Craig then turned to the remaining guards as he walked out the throne room and ordered, "Prepare this room for our guests. We shall return shortly."

One guard immediately turned off the electric lights. Another lit the few candles on the great table.

I followed Craig out of the great room down the long hall. He led me past the door to the cellar, which had just closed as Josh was escorted down the stairs. Craig led me to a room across the hall. The door was closed but unguarded and unlocked.

Upon entry into the small room, I was surprised to see our weapons on a table along with Critter's and Bryan's clothes.

Craig motioned to the table saying, "As a show of trust, you are welcome to gather your weapons, excluding firearms of course. We can't risk an accidental discharge in the middle of the town, as I am sure you are aware."

I studied Craig for a moment to see if he was aware that I was the one who accidentally discharged the firearm causing the zombie horde to attack the camp of the Mountain Warriors. He didn't seem to have made the remark at me personally. I replied, "Those guns are Critter's and Bryan's. I just own the two swords over there."

"Well, go get the swords, then," he said.

I picked them up and slid the scabbards into my belt as Bryan had taught me.

"Wait," said Craig. "Let me see that sword."

I knew which one he meant, but handed him the short sword because I really didn't want another discussion on how I got a hold of a vampire's sword.

"No, no. The more elegant one," Craig said.

I pulled the sword still encased in the scabbard from my belt and handed it to him. He looked over the scabbard and whistled. This was the first time I got to study it closely as well. Everything had happened so quickly from my confrontation with Bryan, to our capture, to having the sword confiscated. I resisted whistling myself.

The scabbard was engraved with caves, confidently postured humanlike figures, bats, stars, and different phases of the moons. The beauty elicited both horror and awe in me.

Craig removed the blade with reverence. The blade whispered to us as it glided against the wooden scabbard. I found that the sound of the withdrawn blade caused me to gasp slightly. There was something about the whisper smoothness that sounded like the blade was grateful to be free and moved through the air like a bird's wing. Craig faced slightly away from me as swung it slowly. I could see an almost childlike awe on his face.

As he swung it, he acquired a smile and started making a "Womp womp," sound as if wielding a light saber from Star Wars. He giggled and then looked worried like an adolescent caught snickering at a funeral service. He then looked serious.

"Beautiful," he whispered as if afraid to wake it. He repeated the word in the same awed whisper a few more times.

He quit swinging it and looked up at the blade as he held it above his head. It was single bladed with a curve, like a katana, to allow devastating slices as Bryan had explained to me yesterday. In a way, I was disappointed. Although the sword was a work of art in its inherent grace compared to the other swords that I had seen so far, the artful engravings of the scabbard were noticeably missing from the sword itself. The sleek blade was strictly for killing.

Craig looked at me and said, "I was afraid the maker of the sword would ruin the blade with the artwork."

"How would art ruin the blade?" I asked.

He gave me a look like I was a fool for asking, "A blade is all business and does not have the luxury of being anything more than that. Any needless engravings would impinge on its strength, aerodynamics, and slicing abilities. It's killing nature is a work of art in itself."

I nodded.

He tapped the edge of the blade and whistled. "Has this ever been used. There's no sign of striking anything hard, like bones."

"I don't know what it's been through before I acquired it, but I slayed two zombies and accidentally struck a rock cliff," I confessed, slightly embarrassed for committing such a sacrilege against the blade.

"Did you sharpen it afterwards?"

"No," I said. "I was captured by your men immediately afterwards."

"Yes, Captain Righter reported that you slew those two zombies, and with quite some skill. It was with this very sword?" he asked.

"Yes."

"Wow," he said, running his finger over it, almost as if caressing a woman's face before a kiss. He added, "I've heard so much about the vampire swords and have only seen them in action from afar. Close up I've only seen them in scabbards. This is such a treat. These sword makers, whoever they were, really knew their art."

"You sound like you're talking about centuries old lore, but these so-called 'vampires' have only been in existence for two years at the most," I said.

"Maybe. Maybe not." He said smiling at me. Too much energy radiated from his eyes. "The plague may have simply reawaken what was widespread centuries ago." He paused and stared at me with wide crazy eyes, "I want it!" he exclaimed as if he desired the whole world.

I was about to ask what he meant, but at this moment I realized that Josh was wrong. Commander Craig was not simply overwhelmed with work and under a lot of stress. With his mood swings from giggling to murderous rages at the smallest slights, I believed that he man was truly insane. I saw him now as a dead end for further questioning, and totally dangerous.

I had so many questions about this world and Bryan and Critter didn't trust me enough to fill me in. I wished I could talk to Josh one more time. I didn't know what he did before or what his educational background was, but Josh had both an intelligent manner about him that hinted at higher education as well as a common sense you see in people with a real world or streetwise background.

"This sword is dangerous for you," said Craig as his eyes lit up on the sword. "People may kill you for such a weapon." He giggled and admitted with serious eyes, "As leader of this town, I would kill you for it myself, but The Specter wants you alive." He giggled and added, "For now."

He then sobered and responded as if he had not just threatened me, "Come now. We have an important meeting to attend."

He placed the sword back into the scabbard, but held onto it. Not with a fighting spirit as Bryan had held it, but rather a childlike reluctance to part with it. That actually scared me more because he was a powerful man, both in physical strength and in command.

I felt a sudden possessive desire to have back in my hands what was mine. That desire overrode my fear of a slightly crazy leader with absolute power. I stepped forward and took the sword from him. I was surprised when he relinquished it with a childlike whine. I placed the weapon back into my belt along with the short sword. The spell that the sword held over him seemed to break. He didn't protest, and his eyes assumed a reasonable brightness. I worried if Abigail had given me an object that attracted the possessor and if the object itself could be used to control someone's mind. I didn't trust her nor the blade, but I didn't feel that I had the power to give it up. I also felt I was being silly and superstitious for thinking such thoughts.

"Let's go," said Craig.

Before leaving the room, I looked through the window and saw that night had fully fallen. Any signs of twilight had evaporated especially in a town devoid of streetlamps. Only fine specks of cold starlight filtered through the bare wind blown branches of the stately poplar trees.

"Are you alright?" he asked.

"I'm fine," I said as I realized that he must have seen the shiver that wracked my body. Although the shudder was quite powerful, I soothed my instincts with the thought that fear of the dark was just superstitious dread. I kept repeating the word, "silliness," that night as I was facing death.

"Let's go," I said firmly and forced myself to follow with a confident stride.

We walked down the dimly candle lit hall. A guard opened the great door to the grand throne room. It took my eyes a moment to adjust to the darkness. The few candles lit the huge room even more poorly than the hallway.

When my eyes adjusted, I immediately focused on them...

Six vampires in their black cloaks with their hoods down stood behind the chairs at the table. Abigail was one of them. She shook her head at me as if to warn me not to do something, but then she just looked off to the left of me. I looked to Richard, the oldest male of the group. He focused his gaze hungrily on me.

"Don't look at him." I heard Abigail say.

I looked at her. She didn't move her lips. It was all telepathic.

"Do not look at me either, but especially do not look at Richard. He wants you. Your very soul, if you believe in one, depends upon you obeying my words."

"What the hell?" I telepathically asked back.

"You chose the right word." I heard her say in my head. The slightest of wry smiles barely cracked her lips, but that hint of a smile was lost to the storm of worry in her eyes.

| 12 |

As Tommy blew out his stress in a breath, his phone vibrated in his pocket. He was about to answer the phone with a curse and a scream when he saw it was Don Renton. Although technically Tommy was the boss, Don had a loose leash and was powerful both in connections and physical strength.

"What's up buddy?" Tommy said into his phone.

"Change of plans," said Don. "The science department has decided--"

"Oh, sorry to interrupt you," Tommy said in a relaxed voice, still leaning back in the uncomfortable chair that cost way too much, "I need to warn you. Captain Josh Righter, of Craigsville's security forces is planning on usurping our man Craig." Tommy knew that Don knew this already so he hoped that the information would simply assure the big man that Tommy was fully on his side.

"Way ahead of you, Mr. Laurens. Anyway, the science department has decided to turn your old friend Eric. The directive has the Governor's approval."

"Wait! What? What do you mean by turn?" Tommy asked, already knowing the answer.

"Turn into a vampire," Don replied.

"I gave no such order," Tommy said. The front of his chair crashed down as he leaned forward.

"The march of science takes priority," Don said with dismissive laugh.

Tommy sat silent as he realized that Don probably had more power than he did. No one had consulted Tommy on a project that he thought was completely under his control.

"Director Laurens?" Don finally prompted.

"How did this come to pass?" Tommy finally asked.

"Richard, the older vampire and the one with the purest virus has requested turning Eric. Eric has responded well to their telepathy. Richard's greatest offspring, your old friend Abigail, will be the one to turn Eric as a test of her loyalty. Richard will take full control of his mind. When Eric agrees, he will no longer be the friend that you knew."

Tommy wiped his hand across his brow and was surprised at how much he sweated. A feeling of worry for his friend concerned him. Even more a worry that Eric would acquire something that neared supernatural power. If he was operating as a vampire in the Forbidden Zone, the Science Department would completely take over. Tommy was losing control over many aspects of his domain.

"This is department overreach," Tommy finally raged.

"It's orders from above," Don said.

"But why would Eric's uncle approve this?"

"Eric's DNA uncannily resembles his uncle's. Their blood-line has proven most receptive to the vampiric virus and the psionic powers that coincide with it. The governor wants that power and sees Eric as the perfect guinea pig."

"This can't happen," said Tommy.

Tommy was surprised when Don hung up the phone with-out saying a further word. Tommy then buried his face in his hands and said, "Eric, what have I done to you, man?"

He looked up into the computer screens and got to work on his keyboard.

***

I stood in the room trying not to gawk at the vampires, particularly Abigail and Richard. Where Abigail talked to me in my head, Richard felt like he was probing my mind with needles of thoughts, but not getting past my defenses. Richard may have been the commander of the vampires, but Abigail was definitely the most skilled, at least with telepathic abili-ties. If this was what Craig dealt with regularly, I could see why he was mad, but as I looked around, I was the only one who seemed to be affected by whatever mind trick was hap-pening.

Richard smiled beneath his hungry eyes and said, "It's good to see you again, Eric. I must apologize for last night."

"No need," I said. "Nothing happened."

My blood suddenly ran cold as the deep thunder of The Specter's laughter rumbled through the throne room. "Fool!" he mocked as he strode towards me and chambered his arm back to beat me down.

The insult felt like a slap across the face. The mere words spoken from such a strong voice felt as solid as the strike that The Specter had knocked me on the ground with just last night. I could almost taste it, an almost burnt, cilantro type taste. I still felt the bruise that he had left on my head.

The Specter swung his fist at me, as I stepped back and to the side. In the same movement, I withdrew my sword and swung it at him just like Bryan had taught. The Specter blocked it as he drew his own sword. We both stood there glaring at each other. Our swords crossed, engaged at a stalemate set to detonate. Each of us awaited the other's next move.

Anger boiled in his eyes as he chuckled. "You think you can best me, human?"

"I don't care," I snarled. "Obviously you need me alive for some reason or I'd be dead already. Strike me again and one of us will die. I don't care who."

His laughter rumbled again. "I almost believed you." He stepped back and sheathed his sword as I still held mine aimed at his face. "Put your sword away, human. You couldn't kill me even if you wanted to, but I like to see that you have some fire in you," he said with a degree of fondness in his voice.

I quickly sheathed my sword, but not before the fearful trembling of the adrenal dump betrayed what truly lay beneath my flash of anger once it burned away. I hoped that no one else had witnessed the tremor.

Abigail's face was impassive, but she subtly nodded her approval.

"Good show," I heard Bryan say behind me. "I see you've ditched your old friends for new."

I looked behind me and saw Critter, Bryan, and Josh standing there with their hands tied behind their backs. I didn't see too much malevolence directed at me. It was mostly directed at the others in the room. Three guards stood behind them with rifles at their backs.

The Specter walked up towards the throne and turned to face us. "We are all among friends. Sit."

Craig and one of his men as well as the six vampires sat at the long table. The Specter stood at the head and motioned for me to sit. I reluctantly sat across from Abigail and Richard.

"Before we start the meeting, let's discuss these three," said The Spector. "Guards, you may go."

The guards nervously looked to Craig.

The Spector's angry voice boomed across the room, "My command is his command!"

"You cowardly bastard, Craig! This is your town!" Josh screamed as his arms tensed against the ropes that bound him.

"Go!" boomed The Spector. "And close the door behind you."

The guards quickly left. A dread swept over me as I realized that whatever happened to Josh, Bryan and Critter, there would be no witnesses other than Craig, who was insane, some literal monsters, and me.

The Spector slowly strode toward the prisoners. I could see the three men strain slightly against their bonds knowing there would be no human intervention coming.

"What should we do with the traitor?" asked Craig.

Richard stood up and followed The Spector. They stood on either side of Josh.

"He is a strong one. His blood is full of vitality. His punishment should be the same as anyone else's." Richard smiled hungrily as he said this.

The other vamps nodded as well. I felt my passionate hatred for them rise up even higher.

"That is not me!" I heard Abigail say, but it was in my head. I made eye contact with her, but she only shook her head so I looked away from her.

"Send him into the woods naked and let us deal with his treachery later tonight," said Richard. I guessed they wanted to do this in the woods because either they held a profane ritual for the bloodletting or it was inconvenient to dispose of the body in the middle of the town.

Josh struggled fiercely against his bonds as The Spector held him firmly by the shoulder.

"Commander! Please!" Josh begged Craig. " No!" Josh was no longer a warrior.

I was filled with horror. I had never seen a man so full of terror in my life. Especially a man who I respected for both his physical and mental strength. I remember the horror in his eyes when he talked about the remains of victims sent to such a fate.

The Specter's laugh rumbled again as he pulled Josh to the great door. He opened it and handed him to the guards. "Take him back to his cell until we release him into the wilds."

Josh screamed in terror as the guards dragged him away.

Richard said, "As my people's population grows, we need more of these prisoners."

"I can't sentence people to death, willy nilly," Craig protested. "I'll have a revolt on my hands. What about Eric Hildebrande. He said that he wasn't with us."

"When did I say that?" I asked.

"The officer's mess hall is bugged. Your conversation with Captain Righter was listened to," said Craig.

"No," said The Specter. "He said that he was with the good guys. He simply agreed so as not to cause trouble with your traitorous Captain. Mr. Hildebrande just needs to be educated on who the good guys are. He doesn't understand the dynamics. He will learn."

The Specter then looked to Bryan and Critter. "So now, let's look at these two, Richard. A more renewable resource. The Mountain Warriors as they call themselves will relieve

Craig of some of the messy business of sentencing so many of his people to death."

Richard walked up to Critter and Bryan smiling like a castaway eyeing a rack of lamb. Critter smiled slightly with a feral look in his eyes. I took the smile to be a nervous reaction. His muscles bunched against the bonds.

Bryan looked stoic, but I could see him sweating against the cold, his breathing increased slightly expanding his chest, but a fire burned in his eyes.

"Relax," Richard attempted a soothing voice that caused my shorthairs to stand. He ran a finger over Bryan's face in the same manner Craig caressed the sword. "These men are wild. Vital. I can smell it in their blood. If your town folk are fat cows, this tribe is full of thriving deer."

Richard walked circles around the two as he inspected them. Occasionally he would touch them like a horse breeder will touch a thoroughbred.

The Specter grabbed them by the back of the collars and yanked down. The cheap jumpsuits ripped down the front exposing their lean, muscular backs and chests. Richard's eyes widened and he ran a fingernail down both men's chest, drawing a few drops of blood from his claw like nails. I could hear all the vampires in the room catch their breaths as they caught the scent of fresh blood. I guessed that vampires had an exceptional sense of smell. The only vampire who didn't react was Abigail. She kept her eyes on me as if worried how I would react.

"That's not me." She didn't say anything, but I heard her.

"That's enough," said Craig, finally speaking out. "I don't have an unlimited supply of jumpsuits!"

The Specter laughed.

"Go to hell, Craig," Bryan growled.

"Don't worry," said The Specter to Bryan. "You are not in danger of death."

Bryan asked, "What about, Josh?"

"This is his last night on Earth because of his foolishness, but we have a deal for you," said The Specter.

"What's that?"

"We will negotiate that while you wait in your cell," said The Specter.

"Negotiate means that we are at the table," Bryan insisted.

"Don't push your luck, human," The Specter warned. He pushed Bryan and Critter out the door and told the guards to take them away to their cells.

The Specter shut the door. When the footsteps of the guards and their prisoners faded down the hall, The skeletal faced man took his seat at the head of the table. and we all sat down. "Now, let's discuss your fate, Eric. I must admit that you proved me wrong. I was told I had to work with you. I saw you as weak. Useless. Your DNA said different. On a few occasions you proved it correct and me wrong. I find you intriguing."

"Do you work for Tommy or my uncle or someone else?" I asked

"I work with many, but for no one," The Specter corrected. "Ultimately, I am the sole authority in the Forbidden Zone as you called it on the outside."

I could hear him saying more, but I felt my head starting to spin. Like I was in a dream falling in an abyss. I could see Richard staring at me intently. I was about to close my eyes to clear my head, when I heard Abigail scream, "Eric! Do not shut your eyes other than for quickly blinking. He is preparing you for the bite that I must deliver to you. He wants your mind under his control when you turn to ensure that you will forever be under his power."

I quickly blinked and looked at Abigail whose eyes were locked on Specter. She closed her eyes. When she opened them she was looking straight at me. She closed them again and looked at The Specter who was still talking. In fact he was arguing with Craig. Richard was now glaring at me. His smugness was turning into frustration. I felt like I was spinning through space again. Again I could feel his needle like thoughts probing at my brain, possibly my soul, trying to get to the depth that Abigail had achieved.

I almost succumbed to Richard's mind when Abigail's voice cut through my brain, "Eric. Do not close your eyes or you will not open them again as a human."

Her face did not move.

I looked at Richard and felt his power over me. Somehow I didn't care.

"Eric. Don't look at Richard. Look at me."

I looked at Abigail.

"Not with your eyes, you fool. He will figure out what we're doing," Abigail's telepathic voice scolded me.

"What?" I asked her back telepathically. I was genuinely confused both by the situation and her words, but I did my best.

"Focus your mind. Look with your mind at my mind."

"You hear me?" I asked.

"Of course. Don't let Richard in," I heard her say.

I started to spin as if falling into the black abyss. I could see nothing but blackness around me. I wasn't seeing with my eyes. I didn't even know if they were open or closed. I felt like days had passed and when I came to I would be far away, free or in captivity. I oddly found myself apathetic.

She somehow cut into my head, "Eric! Stay focused on me. Don't lose it. Look at Richard and confidently shake your head, 'no,' as if you know what he's doing and he won't succeed.

I opened my eyes and saw that I was still in the room, still seated upright at the table.

I shook my head and asked her telepathically, "What?"

"Do it, Eric. Now," her voice commanded in my head.

My head was spinning, but in a slow, pleasant manner. Like a rocker and a lullaby. I wanted to close my eyes and sleep.

"Eric!" Her psionic shout jolted me to my senses.

I opened my eyes and realized a small victory as I saw the smugness on Richard's face. I sat up confidently and shook my head "no," and said, "Hell no," out loud as well.

The smugness dropped off of Richard's face.

"Damn it!" He screamed aloud and smashed his fist into the table. I realized that I answered a question that he had asked out loud, but I hadn't heard. He stood up quickly knocking over his chair. He leaned over the table in my direction.

I was now wide awake. Abigail nodded at me curtly with approval and then looked to the head of the table.

The Specter laughed. "Whatever mind games you two are playing, stop. We have business to finish up."

I thought he was talking to Richard and me, but he was glaring at Richard and Abigail. Was she helping me or was she part of it?

My mind suddenly felt clear. I had started to doubt my sanity for the last few minutes. There was no way I was communicating with her telepathically, I told myself.

I suddenly felt like I was falling through a misty swamp of blood warm mist and water.

"Eric!" screamed her psychic voice in my skull.

The clarity was back.

I looked at Richard and his eyes were burning into my eyes. His face scrunched and intense like he was forcing something.

I started spinning again, but I asked Richard, "Are you constipated or something."

He bared his fangs at me in response, and I heard a faint growl issue from his throat.

I heard Abigail's psychic voice lift me up as my head started to nod off like I was going to sleep, "Eric! Look at The Specter but keep your mental vision on me or they will eat you alive. Yes, Literally!"

I looked at her and blinked

"Don't look at me with your eyes," she scolded with her psionics.

I complied. I saw The Specter looking at me. He was talking to me. The tone of his voice was that of a question? He was waiting for an answer.

"Say, 'yes of course, Specter,'"

I complied and The Specter laughed and said, "Good man."

"Now," her voice in my head said, "Look at Richard and tell him, 'Hell no, blood sucker.'"

It was confusing telling the spoken voices from the psychic ones.

I looked at Richard and laughed at her joke as I said, "Hell no, you wingless mosquito."

"You bastard! I will run you through!" Richard raged. He shot to his feet and drew his sword. I did the same drawing mine.

"Blood sucker," I accused again.

"That's one of ours. Where did you get one of our swords?" Richard demanded.

"For all the pride you have in your power, you really have no clue?" I said. As I held the blade I felt its power like an antennae. I instantly knew that it gave Abigail a channel to my mind and me a channel back to her. The sword was what gave her control over me rather than Richard. I didn't trust her in the slightest, but I trusted Richard even less. My desire was to discard the sword, but I was sure that I would be at his mercy.

"Where did you get that?" Richard demanded again.

"You suck both figuratively and literally at everything you do, don't you?" I taunted. It felt like a weak taunt, but I didn't care. I had to give him all my contempt. I didn't feel completely present, but I instinctively desired to insult him in every way so that I could to keep my control.

I thought he was going to spring over the table to get at my throat. However, Richard and I startled as Specter's voice boomed, "Quiet! Sit down, both of you!"

Richard and I sheathed our swords and sat back down, our eyes never leaving each other's.

"He resisted your head games, eh Richard?" The Specter laughed.

Richard regained his composure and said, "He's pretty good, but this is not over."

"We went over a lot tonight," said The Specter. "Do you have anything to add or any questions about your duties? It's a lot to digest."

I shrugged, not knowing how to reply to his question. I really didn't hear much of anything. I looked at the clock above The Specter's head. I almost swore out loud. Just under two hours had passed in what I thought had been just few minutes.

"Is something wrong?" he asked me. "Do you agree to what was discussed?"

"Uh no. Nothing's wrong. It is, as you said, it's a lot to process," I replied.

"Just tell him yes, but you will think it over," said the woman's voice in my head. She was glaring at me using her eyes to convince me as well.

"Do you agree to what we discussed?" he pressed.

I tried to sound lighthearted as I said, "I guess I really don't have a choice."

"Of course you have a choice. As the Marines say, it's, 'Do or die.'"

"I know. However, I do not wish to be turned tonight. I want to be mentally ready."

"I don't like him," Richard spoke. "He can't be trusted."

I realized if I had blacked out due to Richard's mental tricks, Abigail was supposed to have bitten me. Seeming to have resisted would put me in the upper echelons, maybe above Richard, when I finally did agree to be turned.

"You mean that he can't be controlled by your head games, eh Ricky. That just shows his DNA analysis was correct. As stupid as he appears, he has power," The Specter said.

He now looked at me with a degree of fondness that actually scared me. At this point, I wanted no part of his evil, nor anything to do with the vampires, any of them. I wanted to trust Abigail, but I blamed that on a bad case of ingrained chivalry. Richard was definitely a mind screw, but I suspected Abigail was part of it. Whatever the vamps did to me, it caused me to blackout for a whole two hour meeting, and now she expected me to agree with something, someone, who I wasn't sure was even human. A monster called The Specter who sentenced a good man, in Josh, to be fed to these cannibals.

I looked at the medical equipment piled in front of Richard: blood collection bags, phlebotomy needles, bandages and had a sudden remembrance of what was actually said at this meeting. I was supposed to convince the tribe of Mountain Warriors to give blood to the vampires in exchange for keeping the zombies away from the village. I thought of the thin faces of the survivors. They were already malnourished. Other memories of the meeting seemed to float past, but I was unable to grasp them. All I knew was it was pure evil.

"So what is your answer," asked The Specter.

"In a do or die situation, I choose life of course," I said. I smiled slightly as I became firm in my decision. My way of choosing life may be suicidal, but it needed to be done. I would rather be killed in this horrible world than to comply with his bloody decry. To live as a blood slave, relying on the life fluid from the Mountain Warriors was death.

"Good man!" said The Specter who believed that I had meant to save my own life.

Abigail glared at me. I could tell that she knew that I meant human life against the vampires.

Under the table, my finger caressed the hilt of my sword.

| 13 |

I wouldn't call it bravery to risk my life. I had no choice the way I saw it. I would rather die than to become a monster, and I certainly wasn't going to convince otherwise free people to medically donate their blood to satisfy the vampires in exchange for their lives.

"Good, "The Specter said, assuming I was agreeing with him. "Now—"

I raised my hand and stood up saying, "I hate to interrupt, but I need to use the little boy's room." I used "little boy's room" to purposefully sound as ridiculously harmless as possible. "The food out here is very disagreeable."

"I am sure our vampire friends would agree," Craig said with a giggle. "It is easier to digest fresh blood."

"Of course, you don't need my permission," said The Specter.

"Don't!"

I looked to the source of the psychic voice in my head.

I swore at her harshly in my mind. Her face contorted, and I could see a hint of the true monster that she was.

"Don't! Eric, don't! I know what you are up to. Don't force a hand until we are ready."

"Go to hell, witch! I don't trust you anymore than Richard. I won't try to convince others to feed their blood to you." I mentally shot at her as I turned and left. She may have stopped me from succumbing to Richard's power, but she was still one of them, and I didn't know her game yet.

"Eric, I agree this is horrible, but we can fight this together from the inside. You are dead if you resist. We both are dead," she said.

I opened the great doors and saw that she was starting to follow me.

"Abigail. I must talk to you," The Specter rumbled.

Reluctantly she turned from me and went to The Specter. She gave me one last dirty look and I heard once more, "Do not! You can not save Bryan and Critter," in my head.

As I closed the door behind me I could see both The Specter and Abigail looking at me as the beast spoke to her in a quiet tone. I guessed that I was the subject of the conversation.

As I turned down the hall, my heart sank. There was an armed guard in front of the room with the weapons. That complicated my plan a bit.

"It's the Scribe," the guard announced good naturedly. "You gonna make me famous in your documentary?" He joked, but I could tell that he was also hopeful.

"Yeah, of course, if you can point out the restroom," I said, trying to sound friendly despite suffering from frayed nerves.

"You got it, sir." He turned away and pointed down the hall. "It's just two doors—"

I karate chopped where the base of his skull met his neck like Critter had taught me. The guard immediately dropped to the floor. I had heard about chopping the neck everywhere from martial arts classes to comic books, but I had no idea if it would work or not in real life. I was afraid that I would hit him and he would just get pissed off and kick my ass.

As I dragged him into the room with the weapons, I looked to the heavens and whispered, "Thanks."

I pulled the unconscious guard into the room and quickly gathered up Bryan's and Critter's clothes and weapons and then exited. I tried closing the door all the way but had trouble with all the items in my hands.

"Hey, Scribe," another guard addressed me as he walked my way.

I guessed Scribe was my new nickname in town.

"Yeah?" I answered.

"Have you seen Private Henderson? You know the guard down here?"

"Um, I think he went to the bathroom."

The guard started to look into the bathroom. He pushed the door open a crack.

"Uh, no, the upstairs one," I said, not sure if there was one upstairs. "He mentioned that there was more privacy or something."

"Man, he's skating again. Do you need help with that?" he asked as he approached me.

"No thanks, but could you shut the door behind me," I asked.

I was prepared to attack him if he saw the unconscious guard, but the light in the room was off and the door was already closed enough that he didn't see anything to arouse his suspicion. Without another word the guard bounded up the stairs to check on Henderson.

I opened the door to the basement and walked down the stairs into the gloomy dungeon.

"Who is that?" asked the guard at the bottom of the stairs. It was the same one who was playing the video game.

I peeked over the pile of clothes and weapons that I carried and said, "It's me."

"What are you doing down here?" the guard asked.

"Craig and The Specter told-- ordered me to let your two prisoners go." I said. I could feel my voice quavering.

The guard looked skeptical.

Bryan and Critter still looked angrily at me from behind the bars with their arms tied behind their backs. If I wasn't so afraid of escaping and facing the woods on my own, I would have said, screw 'em, and just saved myself. I know that sounds cowardly and disloyal, but I really had no idea who I could trust at that point. Everyone I knew seemed to be against me.

I said more forcefully to the guard, "The orders come from The Specter. Where they're going is not pleasant."

A hint of fear creased his brow, but he asked, "They get their weapons?"

"Yeah, hold this for me. I have the permission slip in my pocket." I said as I handed him the pile that I carried. I cringed as I said that. "Permission slip" sounded so grade school, but it just came out that way. I wasn't sure of their terminology.

He didn't look like he believed me, but he instinctively reached to hold my burden as I offered it. Once his hands were full, I attacked him with a flurry of punches. None of them landed squarely like the neck chop to the guard upstairs. He continuously moved. My fist kept grazing his face rather than connecting and knocking him unconscious. Both of us fell to the ground: wrestling, kicking, punching. I screamed when he bit me on the ear. I rolled on top of him. As he pulled me to him, I slammed my elbow into his face twice. He immediately went limp.

A strong arm yanked me to my feet and I felt a small but razor sharp knife at my throat.   Critter stood before me and I could smell the smoky and woodsy smell of Bryan, who was holding me from behind.

I held off cracking a joke about him bathing and instead said, "I came to rescue you guys."

Bryan laughed. "You? Rescue us?"

Bryan let go of me, and he and Critter immediately shed their ripped orange jailbird jumpsuits for their own clothes.

"Of course, I have your weapons and clothes," I pleaded. "Where did you get the knife?" I asked.

They ignored me. I was amazed how quickly they switched clothes. I wondered if it was the urgency to escape from this town or the feeling of degradation for these wild men to be confined. Even the prison garb was too much for them.

"You told the guard that you were supposed to lead us to see Craig and The Specter," Bryan shot back.

"I lied to the guard to get you out of jail. I am acting alone."

"And you're telling the truth now?" Bryan said mockingly.

"Obviously, we didn't need your help." Critter added.

I felt rage surge through me. I looked them in the eyes and said, "Listen, I just found out how diabolical they are and how evil their plans are. You guys don't even know."

"We know. Josh told us a lot." Critter said. "It was the confession of a man facing his imminent death."

"Where is he?" I asked.

"They took him to the woods," Bryan said with a dread that caused a shiver in his shoulders.

I swore.

"Yeah," said Bryan.

"His screams when they took him..." The usually stoic Critter was unable to finish as a shudder wracked his body.

They had finished dressing and patted themselves down, double checking to assure that their weapons were within easy access.

"We have to rescue Josh," I stated in a moment of bravado.

"Again, 'we?'" Critter inquired.

Bryan and Critter patted the unconscious guard down and took anything of value. Bryan pocketed a handgun and a spare magazine.

"Guys! What the hell? Why don't you trust me? I'm risking my life, here, with you," I said.

"I trust you. I'm just cautious," said Bryan.

Critter looked me over as if he might find the truth between my head and toes. He nodded and said, "If Bry says so."

"Let's go then," Bryan said, "Keep up, Eric. We'll be moving quickly."

I started to follow Critter up the stairs, but Bryan grabbed my shoulder and stopped me.

"Wait," said Bryan.

What now? I thought angrily. I turned to face him.

"Here. You earned this," Bryan said. "You took him out. It's only fair that it's yours."

I looked down at his hand and saw the guard's handgun and two loaded magazines offered to me. All I knew was that it was a handgun. I didn't even know how many bullets the magazines held.

"Don't shoot it until we shoot. It's on safe. To fire you'll have to press this button, the safety. When the red shows, it's deadly," Bryan quickly explained.

"OK. How do I shoot it?"

Bryan looked at me like I was an idiot. "You point it at who you want to kill and pull the boom switch like Critter taught you last night."

I looked confused.

Bryan smacked me lightly but urgently across the face. "It's not freaking rocket science! You'll get better training later. For now, don't point, even casually, at anything you don't plan to destroy."

"Quit screwing around. Let's go," said Critter as he wore his combat smile, eyes lit with the adrenal rush. The rare times that a smile slashed his usually dour face was when adventure and risk were moments away.

I started to follow Critter as I pocketed the handgun in my coat.

"Keep your firearm in your hand but with the safety on."

I pulled it out and asked Bryan and Critter, "Are your safeties on?"

"Hell no!" said Bryan.

"We're locked, cocked, and ready to rock," Critter said as he summited the steps.

"You might shoot one of us if your finger is twitchy. So keep it on safe unless—" Bryan started to say.

"Yeah, I got it," I said with irritation.

Critter looked out into the hallway from the top of the stairs. "It's clear. Hold your gun at your side, relaxed like you're not armed. Even if a guard sees us, play it casual like we're supposed to be here and that we're going to where we're supposed to go."

I nodded, but I doubted whether I could look so casual under the circumstance.

We walked down the empty hall. I was relieved, but we still had to walk past the great throne room. A sense of dread suddenly hit me. I forgot whether I had closed the doors to the great throne room or not when I excused myself for the bathroom break. I really just wanted to make a run for it. I had to gather up all my discipline to keep my desires to flee in panic under control. I tried to imitate the coolness Critter and Bryan exuded.

Critter strolled to the great room and nodded confidently to me. The door was closed. I started to breathe a sigh of relief, but as I came up beside it, the door unexpectedly opened. The Specter, followed by Craig, nearly walked into me.

"What the hell are you doing?" The Specter's voice boomed through the hallway.

I swore as The Specter drew his handgun from his hip holster.

| 14 |

I was dead if I didn't act. I launched myself at The Specter swinging my right fist up at the tall monster's head. With the stress, I forgot that I held the pistol and the barrel cracked him across the temple. I was stunned to see The Specter fall to the floor.

Craig stood there shocked as well.

For a second, the four of us stared at the blood leaking from The Specter's masked face into the fancy carpet.

Critter snickered, "It bleeds."

"Holy crap," said Craig in a daze. He then looked at us with eyes that quickly cleared as if waking from a spell. "Holy crap," he said again, this time with clarity and urgency. Critter aimed his gun at Craig's head. There was raw determination in Critter's eyes. The gun wasn't pointed at Craig to control him. Critter was in a combat rage and desired blood almost as much as the vampires did. The town's leader was a heartbeat from getting a bullet through the brainpan.

Craig pleaded in a reasonable tone, "Critter, Critter, my friend, chill man. If you kill me, please use a sword. Don't doom my town to a zombie attack. There is a horde nearby."

Bryan grabbed Craig's holstered gun with one hand and reached over with his other hand and lowered Critter's gun arm like pushing on a lever. Critter let the gun descend, but held it ready at his side. Death gleamed in his eyes as his grim smile lit his face.

Bryan said to Craig. "That is entirely up to you, 'my friend.' Let us leave and we don't shoot."

"I can't do that," Craig retorted.

Critter's arm zapped back up with the gun pointed at Craig's head. The smile was replaced by deadly determination to kill.

"Bryan, our kids played together. We know each other. You can't doom my town," Craig pleaded.

"Dude! You're trying to turn us into a vampire smoothie. You doomed your town when you became their slave. Go to hell," Bryan shot back.

Critter's arm tensed as if he took that colloquialism like a literal command.

"Whoa! Whoa! Wait! Wait!" Craig pleaded.

"We're not screwing around. I want to get back to my family," Bryan said, "and you're standing in my way."

"If you shoot me, every soldier in town will be surrounding you in minutes. The Specter will have my head if I let you go, so how about we compromise. I'll give you a five minute head start and no guns."

"Sounds good," Bryan replied with a sense of urgency. I could tell he simply wanted to leave immediately.

As if reading Bryan's mind, Critter pressed the gun to Craig's head as Bryan pushed the town's commander hard against the wall and grabbed some keys from Craig's pocket.

Bryan announced, "We're also borrowing your Hummer."

"Shut up," Critter growled before Craig could protest them stealing his prized vehicle.

"Where'd they take Josh?" Bryan asked.

"We drop off the sentenced convicts at the loop trail under the overlook. You know, Lover's Leap."

"What happened to you, Craig? You pathetic sell out," Critter said.

"Are the vamps in there?" Bryan asked as he kicked open the door to the great room. Critter and Bryan scanned the room with their guns ready. They looked over the room with their guns moving around in line with their eyes--ready to shoot anything that wasn't fully human.

"Let's go," Bryan ordered.

At the moment that we were about to move, six of Craig's guards marched into the hallway. They drew their swords and Bryan, Critter, and I raised our guns. Nervously the guards looked to Craig. The tension was thick. The guards were a split second from dropping their swords and opening up with their rifles even though Critter and Bryan would have lit them up first.

"Guards, let these men pass for now. I need to wake The Specter for orders before we proceed." Craig looked at Bryan, and said, "go."

Craig knelt down and shook The Specter's shoulder as the bleeding monster moaned.

Bryan nodded and the three of us took off at a jog straight toward the six guards. They parted and let us through. Critter purposefully shouldered past a guard who didn't step far enough to the side for the wild man's ego, knocking him into the wall with a reverberating thud that shook the mansion.

Before we exited the building, I turned around for one last look. The Specter was awake and glaring at us from the floor. His eyes pierced me with his unnatural hatred as he shakily got to his feet.

"Get them," he roared.

On the way out of the mansion, Bryan slammed the door shut behind him. From the porch we took off at a full sprint, leaping over the steps. When we were only thirty yards away from a Hummer, the mansion's front door flung open and the guards poured out behind us as we sprinted towards Craig's vehicle.

Four guards stood in front of the Hummer. They started to draw some machetes and swords. They seemed a bit hesitant, not really knowing what was going on. The streets were dark without any streetlights and the guards didn't know who we were. We, on the other hand, had the advantage of knowing that everyone we met was an enemy.

"Swords!" shouted Bryan as he drew his to keep with the truce he made with Craig. I fell behind as I fumbled, pocketing the gun and switching to the vampire sword. Critter threw a knife that impaled the neck of one of the guards. As the guard's hand went to his throat, Bryan's sword beat him and the guard collapsed. Critter and Bryan didn't even break stride and slammed into the remaining three guards, taking two of them out in a blur.

I exchanged a few slashes before I sliced the guard's arm. He dropped his sword, and I ran to get in the vehicle without looking back to see the damage I had wrought. In the darkness, I could see the other two guards in front of me writhing on the pavement--blood gushing from various wounds. Bryan jumped on the hood and ran across it to the other side and got into the driver's seat. Critter took the shotgun seat. I scrambled in the backseat as the big vehicle was already pulling away.

Before I slammed the door behind me, I heard the report of gunfire and bullets smacking into the Hummer.

"What the hell? Are they nuts?" Bryan raged as he gunned the big engine.

"Fricking Specter," Critter growled, "It's not his town. He doesn't care if gunshots get the town overrun by a zombie horde. Hell, the sicko might even see it as entertainment" Critter pulled out his gun. It was no longer a knife fight. "Have your gun out, but keep it on safe," he shouted at me louder than needed to in the excitement.

I looked behind us and saw Craig and his soldiers looking horrified as The Specter aimed down his rifle with grim determination. We turned the corner and I saw our enemies take off in a run, just before a building blocked the view.

"Hey," I said, "I know where there's some *clinmytran*," I said butchering the name of the medicine. I then added, "The antibiotic for bone infections."

"Clindamycin?" asked Brian.

"Yeah, it's at the pharmacy, just up ahead." I said. "There's a window I can bust and probably get it in a few seconds. There it is." Bryan flew past it and turned a corner. "See, they're expecting us," I said.

I looked behind and saw a group of guards step out from behind some trash cans once they realized that we weren't stopping at the pharmacy.

Bryan looked at me in the rearview mirror and said, "Josh told me the officer's chow hall was probable bugged. He told us about another place where we could get some meds."

"How do you know the jail isn't bugged and they aren't set up at the other place?"

"We thought of that, but we mountain boys have our own means of communication," said Critter. "We may wear different jerseys but ultimately Josh and us are on the same side."

"Where are we going?" I asked.

Bryan looked at me again and said. "I'm not saying. This truck might be bugged. The only place I feel safe is in the woods." Bryan's brow knitted with his suspicion of me. "Actually, we never established how Craig and The Specter knew that we were going in the first place."

I blew out an angry breath and returned his eye contact through the rearview mirror. "The same way Craig and the whole damn country knew where you and your family were traversing. Craig and The Specter have access to the drone footage. I can't believe that you haven't figured that out. The drones can obviously pick up conversations, not just video."

"Watch the tone of your voice," Bryan scolded.

"Screw off! I am getting sick of your crap!"

Bryan glared at me for a moment in the rearview mirror like a parent scolding a kid. I returned the stare but said nothing for a moment.

"Listen, I'm sorry, man. I'm just under a bit of stress," I finally said. I didn't feel like I owed anyone an apology, but I really wanted to turn the tension down.

"Stressed? This has been a cakewalk," Critter said in a lazy drawl, breaking the tension, causing Bryan and me to chuckle.

Bryan sighed. He ignored Critter and admitted to me, "Yeah me too, brother. I'm stressed to the max."

"I've been thinking it over. My friend Tommy is pretty high ranking and is in charge of a lot of stuff including the drones. I think he may have control over whoever is in control of The Specter."

"You think so?" asked Bryan.

"Yeah, The Specter doesn't like me and he admitted that I was alive only because someone above him wants me alive." I neglected to mention to Bryan anything about The Specter talking about my blood tests and DNA. For one thing, I wasn't sure if I believed it. Second, Bryan was already weirded out enough about me. I finished with, "Tommy is supposed to send a drone to me to pick up the chip with my video. I'll try to get word to him what's going on. Maybe he can reign in The Specter or pull some strings."

"I guess we'll see whose side your buddy is on," Bryan said.

"You don't trust him?" I asked.

Bryan laughed ruefully, "You do?"

I was too conflicted to reply.

Bryan continued. "This is the guy who got you banished."

"Hey." I started to defend Tommy, but Bryan pushed on.

"This is why I hold back from trusting you. You're a very loyal person and you seem to do what you think is right. However, you're probably the most painfully naïve and gullible person I've ever met and you spread your loyalties too thin."

"That's a bunch of—"

Bryan raised his voice to speak over me, "Your buddy Tommy is in with the same organization that created this plague. And you trust him? Also, that blood sucking witch, Abigail, has you wrapped around her finger."

"Abigail may be on our side," I said. "She helped me--"

"No, she blanked your mind to gloss over her evil."

I couldn't defend her any further. He was tapping into my own doubts.

Critter said slowly, "As the saying goes, you can't serve two masters. You currently want to serve five separate masters. Some of them are very evil."

"I still think Abigail is good at heart."

"Your statement is without evidence," Bryan said.

"You have no evidence to the contrary." I said.

Critter said, "She's a vampire. You'll get your evidence when we get to their killing grounds. I guarantee you that you'll never be the same after seeing it. You won't look at your sweet Abigail the same, I promise. They're all the devil's sidekicks."

I was about to say something in her defense, but Critter turned around and looked at me. His adrenaline induced smile was gone. I could see in his eyes the horror that he must have seen when he saw the victims of the vampires. When I closed my mouth, he nodded grimly. Sometimes Critter could say more without words than most people could write in a book.

I noticed that Bryan drove in a circle around a white brick building.

"We're clear," said Critter.

I noticed it was a pet shop. "What's up?"

"You can get antibiotics for pets without a prescription. Josh said there was a stash here that others weren't aware of," Bryan said as he parked the vehicle.

Critter jumped out before the Hummer came to a stop. I opened the door and Bryan yelled, "Keep your ass in the vehicle."

But I had already jumped out.

Bryan shouted, "Stand guard, but as soon as Critter's back with the antibiotic, we're gone. If you're not in the vehicle, you have a long walk ahead."

I drew my gun and watched Critter easily jimmy the back door. He dashed into the store. I could see his flashlight jumping around on the walls through a window. Then the light came to a halt. Then it bounced a final time and the light shut off.

Moments later, Critter burst through the door and slammed it behind him. As he raced for the Hummer, The Specter sprinted around the corner of the building behind Critter followed by a few of Craig's guards. The Specter stopped and shouldered his rifle to shoot at Critter.

Without thinking, I flipped off the safety and aimed in Critter's general direction. Critter's eyes widened and he ducked, but he headed straight at me in a combat crouch. I thought he was about to tackle me. I squeezed the trigger hoping I was aiming high enough over his head to miss but low enough to still hit The Specter or the guards.

I saw chips fly off the corner of the white brick pet shop from the impacts of my bullets just slightly above The Specter's head, causing him to back up behind the corner.

"My gun quit shooting!" I yelled in panic as I kept pulling the trigger with no effect.

Critter jumped in the already moving Hummer. "I got the antibiotics. Move!"

"Get in! You're outta bullets," Bryan yelled at me.

I know that sounds stupid, but that was the first time I had ever been in a gunfight. I found that I had trouble counting my own bullets when someone was shooting bullets back at me, to put it mildly.

Bryan had already floored the gas pedal. I stumbled as I raced to get in. I held onto the door frame as my feet dragged on the ground. I was almost forced to let go.

"Stop, Bryan!" Critter yelled.

He slammed on the brakes and my head smashed into the open door.

"Get your ass in!" Bryan screamed at me.

I could hear the bullets smacking into the vehicle as I got a leg inside. Bryan hit the gas before my other leg could be pulled in. The sudden acceleration caused the door to slam on my leg.

I swore at the pain and yanked in my remaining leg. The door slammed again. This time it closed tight.

Bryan made a few quick violent wrenches of the wheel as he navigated the streets. He yanked the wheel and aimed the Hummer on a collision course with the main gate. A few guards stood in front of it and aimed rifles at us.

"They ain't screwing around." Bryan swore.

"Duck." Critter advised.

I brought my head down and could hear the bullets pinging off the engine, shattering the windshield and whistling through the interior above me.

Bryan cursed the guards. Critter laughed at fate. Critter ducked down beneath the dashboard. He made eye contact with me. They were lit up like spotlights. This wasn't nervous laughter. This crazy bastard was enjoying getting shot at.

Peering an inch above the dashboard, Bryan yelled, "Hold on gents. Be ready to exit and fight if we don't make it through!"

With my head almost on the floorboards, I couldn't see ahead. The bullets quit pinging off of the engine block so I guessed the guards jumped out of the way.

We smashed into the sturdy barn door. All the supports for the gate were designed to keep others out rather than in. Even so the Hummer halted with a crash and I slammed into the front seat.

The big engine stalled. The barn door lay strewn in shattered pieces around us. We were surrounded by the guards whose bullets started sacking the vehicle. Critter opened the door and started shooting.

| 15 |

"Come on!" Critter ordered as he started to exit the Hummer with his gun at the ready..

"Hold up!" Bryan screamed as he cranked the engine. The Hummer grumbled and complained and then the ignition caught. Critter got back in and slammed his door as I heard at least three bullets smack against it.

"Hold on!" Bryan yelled and floored it.

The hummer launched but without the power it had earlier. I could smell diesel in the air.

As we left the town behind, Critter laughed and smacked the dashboard. "Ole Craig's gonna freak when he sees what we did to his ride."

Bryan laughed. His laugh was a bit of a sigh of relief. "Serves him right. He needs to learn how to be a better host, but he'll see it soon enough when the zombies arrive to check out the noises." It was silent other than the rumbling diesel engine until Bryan swore, "Gents, we're about out of juice. I think they shot a fuel line."

That was prophetic. Immediately the engine started chugging. We were less than a quarter mile from the town.

Bryan turned off the road, downhill into the forest, and the engine died on its own as we coasted downhill into some brush and came to a stop with a crash against a sturdy tree.

"Out," Bryan ordered.

Critter was already out. As Bryan and I turned to run to the road, Bryan stopped and said, "What the hell? We don't have time for this crap."

I looked and saw Critter, peeing on the floorboard. "As a man of few words, I thought this would let Craig know how I feel."

Critter zipped up and started towards us.

"You forget something?" Bryan asked.

"Oh yeah," Critter said. He reached back in the car and pulled out a small plastic bag with what I guessed were the antibiotics. "Dang it! I got some piss on the bag."

"You idiot," Bryan said.

"Did you get the receipt?" I asked.

Critter looked confused for a second and said, "Shut up, man." He was done laughing.

We ran up and stopped at the road. From that vantage point, it looked like the Hummer was hidden enough from a quick drive by in the dark, but it would easily be found in the daylight.

"Come on!" Bryan ordered as he rushed to the other side of the road. "They're coming!"

We dashed into the bushes on the other side of the road. The headlights of three vehicles washed over our tense faces, but either we were deep enough in the forest or they must have been in too much of a hurry to catch Craig's Hummer. I gasped as I swore that I made eye contact with The Specter, who rode in the passenger seat of the same van I had ridden in earlier with the tell tale whine from hitting the zombies.

But The Specter didn't see me. He was as mortal as me, I told myself.

We stood still for a moment after they passed like we were afraid somehow they could hear us move.

"Breathe," Bryan told me. "Your body is freaked out enough. Don't add asphyxiation to its list."

I let out my breath and felt my shoulders relax.

"Besides, you'll need your breath for the run we are about to make," said Critter.

Without saying anything, Critter took my handgun and reached in my pocket and grabbed the spare magazine and loaded the full mag for the spent one.

"We got a long run ahead of us," Bryan agreed.

"You think they can find us?" I asked.

"Hell no," said Critter. "We rule the forest. I'm just not sure about your vampire girlfriend." Critter chambered a round in my handgun and handed it back to me after he made a show of flicking the safety back on.

"However, I want to save Josh, if I can. He's a good man," Bryan said.

"Yeah, Josh is a good man," Critter said, "but I wouldn't wish death by vamps even on a traitorous ass like Craig."

"But Eric's vampire friends are just misunderstood," Bryan quipped.

"Especially the purdy one," Critter added.

"Dude! I'm with you guys. I'm being hunted just like you. By my choice!" I said. I could feel anger raising into my face like a tide.

"Relax. We're joking," Bryan said, but didn't look like he was joking.

"Cutting the tension with humor. The tension is thick with you," Critter said with a slap on my shoulder. "Besides, as far as blood suckers go, she ain't bad to look at."

"I'm not as naive as you guys think! Abigail--"

Bryan cut me off and warned, "Just watch it. A pretty face can hide a heart as black as The Specter's. In fact, it can be worse because you're so blinded by infatuation that it ambushes you."

"I got it. Just don't treat me like I'm stupid."

"Enough talk, brothers," Critter said as he turned to jog up the hill through the brush. He took point man as usual.

I got into the routine that had already been established and fell in behind Critter as Bryan covered the rear. The hill looked like it was just short of a sheer cliff. I didn't know how trees or anything felt comfortable, not just growing but thriving on such a steep face. It inspired awe in me. I included the Mountain Warriors in that disbelief and respect. They seemed to thrive anywhere, even when hunted like animals.

Bryan spoke to me as we ran, and I could barely hear him above the crunch of the leaves under my boots and my heavy breathing,

"We'll stick with swords from now on. I'm guessing we won't be followed up to the vamp's feeding area through these woods. Craig won't want his troops to see the remains of the vampire's dinner. It may lead to open revolt."

"I hope you're right," I said, and I thought anyone who would try to pursue these armed, human mountain goats through these hills had to be off his rocker.

Critter hissed over his shoulder at Bryan and me, "Quiet. Zombies respond to human voices."

Between stumbling through the rooty, rocky hills and getting whacked by tree limbs, I had time to think and mentally digest some of what I'd seen and heard earlier when Abigail and Richard seemed to blank my mind. Parts of the meeting with The Specter came to haunt my memory. Abigail's mind games didn't blot that out completely if that was her intention. I was still confused as to whether she was helping me against Richard or if that was their combined game against me. She was a hell of a conundrum. I was even debating whether to ditch the sword that she gave me.

Actually, she shouldn't have been a conundrum at all if I used my rational sense. She was just like The Spector or Richard, and I wouldn't trust that blood sucker at all. If it was Richard who screwed with my mind to protect me from Abigail, I would consider it a mental violation of the worst form.

However, her deep eyes and innocent looking face (innocent when not angry) made me doubt my rationality. Were the eyes indeed the windows to the soul as they say? If that was true, a better question would be, could the soul lie as easily as the tongue? I mean, she was a literal monster, a vampire, in the truest sense of the word. Her face, when angry, betrayed what was truly in her heart. Her beauty was a mask. I reasoned that normal people wear monster masks to scare others. Monsters on the other hand wear human masks to lure us in. I could not let her fool me again.

"Eric," she said clearly.

I looked around the woods and realized it was her voice in my head again.

I mentally cursed her back. I still looked around as I wondered how far she could communicate in this manner. Before it had happened when we were almost within arm's reach of each other. I didn't think that she could influence me outside of visual range.

"What's the matter?" asked Bryan in a harsh whisper from behind me.

"Nothing," I said out loud.

I realized I had stopped marching and stood still to look for her. Critter stopped as well to look at me. He walked back to me, sensing that something was wrong.

I heard her again. "Eric, don't curse me. I am not near you, but you are nearing our stronghold. Tell your friends to go back."

There was a bit of urgency in her voice. I didn't know why. Was it for my safety or hers?

"Josh. We're here to save Josh from you—you monsters," I replied back to her telepathically.

"Eric, don't call me that," she said in an offended voice. I could see her in my head with her red lower lip protruding forward in the cutest pout. I could not fall for that!

No, I told myself and then to her I said, "Monster!"

"What's the matter with you?" asked Bryan.

I realized I said, "monster," out loud. "Nothing. No, it is something bad. We're nearing their territory. The vamps."

"What?" asked Bryan.

I heard her loud and clear shouting in my head. "Don't tell your friends anything. They will doubt your sanity and loyalty. Just leave the area."

I looked at Bryan. I straightened my posture to try to look in control, sane, and said, "I hear her thoughts. She's warning us of danger."

"To hell with her. This is our woods. We're the ones who should be feared!" Critter declared as he looked in the direction that we were headed.

Bryan added, "She just doesn't want you, her white knight, to see the bloody handy work of her and her friends."

In the night, the solid black shadow that was Critter's form, stopped and turned around.

"Can she locate us with you?" Critter asked as he walked up to me and looked me straight in the eyes.

"I don't think so. I can block her." I was telling the truth. I felt that I could place thoughts in different compartments in my head. Some of them I could isolate and lock from her. Although, I also felt that I carried a physical part of her in a physical part of my brain near the right side of my forehead. Although I couldn't rid her from my mind, I could isolate her from the rest of it.

Critter looked at me as I considered something. I looked at him and said, "There are three maybe four other vampires with her. They're looking for Josh. She's the only one of them who knows that we're close by."

I pointed twenty degrees to the left of where we were going. "They're about a mile and a half ahead." I pointed to the right and said, "Josh is about to be dropped off a mile that way."

I heard her psychically scream hideously in my ear and then I felt her presence in my head leave.

"Baloney," Bryan hissed.

Critter considered the direction that I pointed. "Eric's right. The drop off point for the condemned is in that general direction. That's if Craig was telling the truth of it being at the trailhead for the loop trail. We've been turned around a bit, but I do know this area enough to know that Eric is right."

Bryan glared at me. There was no way I could humanly know the direction and the distance to the drop off point. We all knew it.

Bryan said, "Eric, I believe that deep inside you're a good man, but as I said, you're too naïve, way too naïve. No offense."

I cringed as he stepped up to me. His nose almost touched mine. "I hate to do this," he said as he reached in my pocket and pulled out the handgun. "You can keep the swords, but I don't know if you're possessed, insane, or on the level. Until I know for sure, I don't trust you with a weapon that can reach me outside of my sword strike."

"Possessed?" I said each syllable slowly. It was not a word I ever thought I would hear used in a serious conversation, especially not in reference to myself, but I had felt her in my brain. I had to admit that that had to be a form of possession. I wished for some way to blow away whatever it was that was in my head. I actually understood one of the final scenes in the book Fight Club. .

"Listen," Bryan said, "Although I'm a Christian, I never took that word, possessed, that seriously. However, I never took zombies, vampires and all the other spawn seriously either. If she's speaking in your head, and you aren't insane, we really can't rule anything out."

I nervously asked, "You said 'other spawn.' There's more out here?"

I heard something, an animal, howling in a yipping high voice as the full moon burst through the clouds. After running in the darkness the moonlight lit the mountain forest up almost like daytime.

"Don't tell me there are werewolves," I begged.

Critter cocked his head to listen to the distant howls and cracked one of his wry grins. "Not them. Those are just coyotes. A real werewolf's deep throated howls makes the coyote's howl sound like Chihuahua's yips in comparison."

I was visibly shaken.

He grinned even bigger in the moonlight, and I couldn't tell if he was enjoying putting me on or was excited at the thought of sword fighting with a fricking werewolf.

I looked to Bryan to see if he would let on whether Critter was telling the truth or putting the new guy on. Bryan just looked grim, then said seriously, "We have distance to cover and a friend to save. Let's get moving."

Critter acknowledged him by turning his back to us and setting the running pace without a further word.

Within a moment of running we saw headlights far above in the mountains, about a mile ahead in the direction where we were heading. We exchanged grim looks. Josh was getting dropped off. Critter increased the pace of the run to almost a full sprint. We followed closely.

I was quickly winded. Every muscle in my body ached from the assault I had placed it through in the last three days. Although the break in the run felt good in the moment, it allowed everything that was bunched up to stretch. It felt like my body had to go full tilt or nothing until we got back to my tent to sleep for the night.

The moonlight made the run a little easier. We still bushwhacked with nothing even resembling a trail in sight. Critter took us on his own path and we splashed through a small creek up the mountain. I cursed my soaked socks and boots. We weaved around and over boulders and rock faces. Countless branches smacked my face.

My head was silent as I fell into the trance of the run. Both my worries and the voice of the vampire girl were gone. The rhythm of the run soon solely occupied my tired mind. I eventually forgot my exhaustion as the rhythm of my tread became my whole existence.

I seemed to come back into my body as Critter raised a hand in the air and stopped running. He walked forward and made some hand signals over his shoulder without looking back at us.

Bryan crept up and translated the hand signals by whispering in my ear. "There's a trail about five meters ahead running perpendicular to our direction." He pointed up into the canopy of the trees. "Do you see the break in the trees?"

I followed his finger and nodded. The branches on the trees were densely packed together. Then, a little ahead of Critter, I saw a break that formed a line of open sky as far as I could see on either side of me.

Bryan said, "This trail is an old logging and fire road."

Critter led the way and we crept forward and made it to the trail. We came to a halt at its edge. We were now on the top of a ridge that led to another towering ridge a few hundred meters above us. Sometimes I wondered if there was ever a ridge or peak that was the highest. Every trail upwards seemed to lead to another higher ridge or summit.

"What's up?" asked Bryan looking back and forth down both directions of the trail.

"We're close, but I'm not sure which way we go," Critter said.

"We need to go to the right," I said as I confidently pointed. I reacted without thinking and now I had to suffer the skepticism. Sometimes, I wished I could keep quiet.

"You sure?" asked Bryan.

I hesitated in answering.

Critter nodded as he sniffed the air, "He's correct."

"How do you know," Bryan asked.

A shudder went through Critter. "I caught a whiff of the dead."

In the cold air I caught the faint scent of decay.

Critter made eye contact with me and held it for a moment before embarking on the trail. We were no longer running but rather walked slowly, quietly on the leafless trail. I kept a sharp eye on him. Every time Critter stopped and raised his hand, Bryan and I would stop and listen.

However, other than the whisper of the light breeze through the trees and the occasional yips of the distant coyotes, the night was silent.

But all of us knew we were far from being alone in the woods this moonlit night.

"Hold on to your tummies, boy." Critter muttered. "We're close."

***

Annoyed, Tommy held the phone almost a foot away from his ear. He sat at his desk staring at the ceiling. A video game was on the computer. He brought the phone to his mouth and said, "I'm searching right now." After he said that he moved the phone a foot away from his ear again.

"How can you not find them?" The Specter's booming voice screamed through the speaker. In the background Tommy could hear a big diesel engine rumbling as well as a whine from a slight mechanical problem.

Tommy replied, "Relax. I--"

"No!" This time Tommy held the phone at arm's length as The Specter screamed, "You do your job and I-- we can relax!"

"I think your vampire chick is interfering or something," Tommy replied.

"She is nowhere near. Your friend knocked me unconscious! He is only alive because of his uncle! But that is no guarantee. Things happen out here!"

Tommy sat up straight. The Specter was known for his rages but this went far beyond anything that Tommy had seen in the past.

"I'm working on it now. I should find them in a moment. I would keep driving on that road if I was you."

"Call me when you know anything worthwhile."

Tommy opened his mouth to reply, but The Specter had hung up.

Tommy placed his phone away and clicked on the computer. The game disappeared and a shot of the woods appeared. There was only the slightest hint of green background from the advance night vision technology. He smiled as he watched Eric, Bryan, and Critter carefully stalk along the trail.

The drone that he was using was a personal drone that could not be tracked. No one would know that he knew about Eric's whereabouts.

Tommy was actually proud of his friend. It had hurt him watching Eric waste away on alcohol knowing that his friend strived for more. That degeneracy was far worse than dying doing your purpose on this planet, Tommy reasoned. Yeah, he dealt a bit underhanded by lying through omission, and yes, Tommy was dating Eric's ex-girlfriend, but Eric was really surprising everyone in the government. Eric had some metal in him.

On the other hand, yes a documentarian turned vampire would be awesome for ratings, but there was no way Tommy would let Eric get turned unless he was sure that Eric would not get killed or mentally deranged in the process.

Tommy panned back on the drone, getting a wider view. He swore as he realized that the trail was leading to the vampires' feeding ground. He cursed again as he panned out further and noticed a blip on the screen signaling another drone in the vicinity. Tommy switched to that drone and buried his head in his hands in defeat.

A large coven of black cloaked vampires were headed toward Eric and his two friends. Even worse, clicking on the drone footage would leave a digital fingerprint.

Tommy waited a minute giving Eric as much time as he could before he dialed The Specter. Tommy held the phone away from his ear in anticipation.

"What!"

Tommy spoke into the phone. "I just found him. They ditched the Hummer and are far off the road. They'll be at the mercy of the vampires in a matter of moments."

| 16 |

We continued on the slow, almost stalking walk for another hundred meters when Critter stopped. He raised a
hand. Bryan and I stopped as well. I barely heard Critter hiss
an oath. Although it was a quietly hurled profanity, I could
hear the anguish in his heart. I crept up next to him and swore
as well when I saw the body.

It was long dead, but it wasn't just lifeless, it was like the
vitality of what made him human had been sucked out of him,
and I guess that was a correct assumption considering who the
murderers were. The corpse stared at us with eyes and mouth
agape. The mouth opened in a silent scream unheard except
deep within my heart. The glassy eyes accused us of not res-
cuing him from the obvious horror of vampirism. With the
color of vitality literally drained, the skin was a deathly pale in
the harsh moonlight. I saw the dark gape in the neck where
his life had left him. The cold of winter gave some preserva-
tion to his death.

DEADLY ALLY - 223

The accusing ghost of this man would forever haunt my dreams.

Oddly, I sighed in relief. Once I overcame the initial horror, I realized that this wasn't Josh.

Without saying what he saw, Critter either pointed or touched the corpse with the sword's tip. I realized he was pointing out evidence of who did this, what happened and how. His sword tip touched: The hands bound behind his back. The gaping hole at his throat. Something about the face that I didn't understand. The footprints surrounding the corpse. Something on the ground that I couldn't see. We already knew who did this, but there was some mountain justice in officially pointing out the evidence. We were free to exact our justice upon the vampires.

Critter turned from the corpse to look at us. We stood in a triangle and looked wordlessly at each other. We were so sickened. We could see the mutual lust for slaying vampires in each other's eyes. It was a bond between the three of us that need not have been spoken. As I said, there comes a point where desire for what is right overrides the desire to live, and I didn't want to live in a world where this was a reality.

Bryan nodded at me and took something out of his pocket. He handed me my handgun.

"You trust me?" I asked.

He shook his head and replied, "Not entirely, but I'd risk a bullet in my back to ensure you or another human doesn't end up like this poor bastard."

I shivered as he spoke those words.

"Stick with swords. Don't shoot unless we start shooting," Critter instructed. "We're nearing the ridgeline that overlooks the valley of our village. We don't want to attract anything else."

"Can we bury him?" I asked. It felt like a betrayal to leave that man with the horrified look and accusing eyes to rot even more in the open air.

"As the saying goes, 'Let the dead bury the dead.' We can only protect the living. Let's find Josh," Critter said as he took off at a quicker walk. He was still stealthy, but there was a sense of urgency that quickened as the scene unfolded.

We came upon more bodies as we followed that revolting section of trail. Each body was equally as horrifying as the first, but instead of getting used to it, the effect of the carnage amplified exponentially in my head. It was like seeing a collection of dead bugs beneath a spider's web, only these were people like me who once had dreams. The stench, even on this cold winter night, became almost overpowering. We were all breathing through our mouths to limit the smell. However, it seemed the stench became embedded on my tongue. I dry heaved once.

"Easy," Bryan said with grim compassion and a comforting hand on my shoulder.

The corpses were strewn all over. It reminded me of a rough part of town for vampires. Instead of seeing liquor bottles and heroine needles strewn along an alleyway, there were human corpses, used up and disposed carelessly as if in a drunken orgy. I grew more terrified with each step.

Oddly, my companions seemed only more enraged. Their heads were held higher as if desiring to raise the level of human dignity despite the wickedness we witnessed. Their shoulders were squared. Drawn and ready swords were clenched in all three of our fists. Bryan and Critter wanted a fight far more desperately than mere safety.

It rubbed off on me. The only difference was that they seemed completely resolute on the destruction of the monsters. On the other hand, I was emotionally all over the spectrum of human feelings. I would feel a surge of bravado and ten seconds later I felt an almost paralyzing fear. In fact, Bryan occasionally had to poke my back with his sword to remind me to walk forward.

Critter stopped in the middle of the carnage. He looked at the trail and started to chuckle. What could be so funny, I wondered. Had the mountain man finally lost his marbles in the face of these atrocities. The thought of my protectors losing their minds horrified me to the core. Had I not felt the blood pulse pounding in my throat, I may have wondered if my heart had stopped as I stood locked in place.

Bryan pushed past me as I found myself frozen in my steps. He rushed up to Critter, "What?" he demanded of Critter.

"Our man, Josh, is running free. Armed and dangerous as they say," Critter said, still chuckling. He nodded his head as he studied the ground.

I didn't know how he knew. I looked around at all the gaped mouth witnesses, the corpses. They said nothing of what happened to Josh here. They just bespoke of their own horrendous end.

Critter pointed his sword at the ground and walked us through what he saw. He spoke in a clipped language as his brain power seemed to be focused more on the story of the events rather than language and syntax of the telling of it.

"Tire tracks," he whispered. "Josh led out by two men." Critter's sword pointed the way as he said, "Must have kicked one of them in the face. Choked the other with his rope." Critter chuckled with admiration of the escape. "He escaped his bonds." He pointed where one set of boot prints stood behind another. The one in front had pressure marks on the heels where he was pulled back by the man choking him from behind. Even I could see it once it was pointed out to me.

Critter laughed and pointed into the woods where I could see some cord.

He continued the narration. "There's the rope. The choked guy got away and crawled there. Josh let him go. Must have got what he wanted." Critter squatted and looked closer at the ground. "Choked man crawled here and spat in the dirt. Blood in the spit. Josh kicked his ass. Ran." Critter pointed into the forest. "The whole crew drove away. The driver is the fourth set of boot prints. Can see him helping the others back in. They will all live."

"How do you know that Josh is armed and not wounded?" asked Bryan.

Critter stood up and spoke normally, "He'd be dead if he didn't have a weapon. There is no way he'd just run into vamp, zombie country unarmed and without a fight. Also, Josh is a bad ass. His men would have feared going toe to toe with him. They'd rather run. Also, we didn't hear gunfire and the men, as much as they feared Josh, they also respected him.

They would not purposely maim Josh to make him a better victim. They would want to give him a fighting chance or a mercy bullet through the back of the skull. Even tied up his men would want him to have a chance against the vamps. I wouldn't be surprised if the men untied him as a favor, and Josh whooped their ass for their kindness." Critter chuckled. "Josh is a great guy. I hope he heads to our village."

"Should we look for Josh?" I asked, looking into the woods where Critter had pointed his escape.

"No, he's got a head start and I can't trail him that fast through the leaves at night, even with the moonlight."

"Will he be safe?" I asked.

"Safer than us," Critter explained. "We're more likely to end up on the vampire's dinner plate than he is." The dour man sounded relatively upbeat. Then in a grim tone he said. "Now we have to worry about getting the antibiotics back to camp for Peter. And I hope we find out that you saved Tomas with the red hot coffee pot. Burning him was savage. Be good if it works."

I nodded. I had, for a moment, forgotten the reason why we were on this trail. This morning and all that happened through the day seemed like a year ago, and we weren't close to being done.

"Let's go," said Bryan.

Critter turned to go when I distinctly heard the woman's voice in my head ordering me to, "Hide!"

I reacted by grabbing Critter's shoulder and almost pulled him in the brush. Seeing my insistence, he cooperated. Bryan followed. I placed a finger to my lips before either could question me.

We waited, ducked in the brush. A corpse sat propped up in a sitting position against a tree. In my squatting position, it stared at the side of my face a few inches away. I could smell its stench as we waited, but I didn't feel safe enough to move to a comfortable distance from the corpse.

Bryan opened his mouth to protest waiting, but Critter raised a finger as his head was cocked to the trail. Another moment went by and I saw Bryan shift irritably. His patience was over. He wanted to be back in the village with his family, friends and his duties, but he settled down, probably out of respect to Critter's instincts.

I felt my blood cool twenty degrees. I then shuddered as I watched five cloaked and hooded figures walk toward us. The corpse that stared at me from a foot away seemed to want to scream an accusation at those creatures. I desired to be his vengeful spirit.

The vampires walked up and as they walked past looking straight ahead, my blood seemed to drop even lower in temperature. One of the hooded forms turned slowly and looked straight into my eyes.

It was her. As she turned, I caught a look at her face in the moonlight. Her eyes were so soulful. I didn't want to believe she was capable of what the corpse beside me seemed to cry out about.

A finger slowly came to her lips. Apparently, she was the only one of the vampires who knew we were there. I guessed that was either due to our psionic connection or maybe the accursed sword. In another couple seconds we would be safe. They walked on.

Critter stood up.

I heard Bryan curse the tracker under his breath, "Damn. Critter. Here he goes."

"The hell I'll be quiet, witch!" Critter shouted at the group, specifically at Abigail. Critter motioned us to be quiet with his hand. He stepped boldly onto the trail, sword pointing at them.

The vampires turned together slowly to look in his direction. These were apex predators who only saw us as food. None of them showed any fear except Abigail. In fact, they seemed shocked that someone would be so foolish as to call on them.

"You should have stayed quiet," Abigail said in my head.

"Sorry. That's Critter for you." I told her in my mind.

"You should have run," her voice in my head told me. "Your friends will be killed and I will be forced to turn you."

Bryan pushed past me to stand shoulder to shoulder with Critter. Bryan said over his shoulder to me, "Watch our backs. This ain't gonna be pretty."

"Who says it won't be pretty," asked Critter with his adrenalized grin.

I looked down and saw the vampire sword in my hands. I couldn't remember drawing it. As scared as I was, I was ready for whatever came.

Richard looked out from his hood. He smiled smugly and tauntingly replied. "You fools. I would have thought—"

Critter screamed a war cry of pure fury and bloodlust and flew at them, particularly Richard, but it was clear his desire was to level the whole coven. The clang of steel rang out into the night as Richard brought his sword out to block the attack. Bryan and I ran to follow him. Critter's berserker mentality found him surrounded, but he was a whir of lethal steel. Bryan and I fought our way to him so a vampire could not run him through from behind. We formed a triangle facing out as the vamps gracefully circled us, all the time exchanging ringing slashes with our swords.

In the swirl of battle I found myself facing off with Abigail.

"You should have run, Eric." I heard her in my mind as I deflected a downward slash from her. I considered the irony that my block was with the sword she had given to me earlier today. However her slash lacked fire. I could tell that she was holding back.

I thought of making a cheesy remark about how I just had to see her, but instead, I slashed across at her face.

"Talk to me Eric," she said in my head as she ducked the swing of my sword..

I ignored her plea. I didn't even respond with a curse. I stepped to the side and blocked as her sword came at me from a diagonal downward slash.

"Where is this fog coming from?" Bryan screamed. I could hear panic rising in his voice. He was breathing raggedly and his sword strikes faltered as if unsure.

Critter cursed with frustration. He was swinging wildly and hitting nothing. His opponents backed up as the circle of vampires widened. Both of my companions had their eyes closed.

I glared at Abigail who said in my head, "I warned you."

I could feel myself getting woozy, but I refused to close my eyes.

I yelled above the fray, "Bryan! Critter! Keep your eyes open! The fog is an illusion!"

Critter swore back at me.

Suddenly I was engulfed in the fog. As the fog hit, one of the vamps took advantage. I couldn't see him, but I saw his sword slashing down at me. I was barely able to block. My breath was ragged. It was hopeless, but I forced myself to fight back. I pressed back at my opponent and caught a glimpse of his intense face.

It was Bryan swinging at me with his eyes closed, but moving his head looking around as if his eyes were open.

"Bryan! Open your eyes! You are attacking me!" I screamed at him.

He swore as he opened his eyes, saw me, changed his angle, closed his eyes again and began swinging blindly. Steel rang heavy on steel again. It sounded like cymbals crashing in a chaotic fast rhythm from a death metal song.

I opened my eyes wide and the fog disappeared. The vampires circled us from a distance and simply watched us fight each other. At each others' throats, Critter's and Bryan's eyes were closed and clenched They grappled in mortal combat. Each one grasped the wrist of the other's sword arm. All the vampires were smiling smugly, watching us attempt to kill each other. All except Abigail.

Abigail looked straight at me with pity. From the front of my mind I heard her sweet voice, "I tried to warn you. More of us are coming. Leave your friends. They are already dead. Run."

I kept my sword pointing at the vampires to keep them at bay as I went to break up my fighting friends.

"Critter! Bryan! Open your eyes. You're fighting each other!" I screamed, but they were too engaged in deadly combat to hear me. Or they were too deep into the spell of the vampires.

Critter dropped his sword and grabbed one of his hidden knives from his sleeve with his left hand. I ran up and grabbed his knife hand with one of my hands. With the other hand, I kept my sword pointed out and my peripheral vision on the vampires.

"Critter! You're about to kill Bryan." He didn't heed.

Bryan removed a bowie knife from Critter's belt and was about to stab Critter.

"Scream with your mind at them like you do with me. It's an electric mental impulse. It will penetrate the spell." Abigail said in my head.

I yelled at them vocally and mentally. I continued to mentally scream as I slapped Bryan across the face even as Bryan's acquired knife went at Critter's throat. Bryan opened his eyes. He tried to pull back, but he gouged Critter's neck pretty badly.

Critter roared and attacked wildly as Bryan yelled Critter's name over and over.

I physically pushed Critter away and screamed at him in my mind. He fell and rolled to the ground and opened his eyes. He came to a stop at Richard's feet. Richard's sword came down towards Critter's face. I thrust my sword above Critter just in time to prevent the deadly strike from cleaving the tracker's skull.

Critter came to his full senses and rolled back, coming to his feet next to Bryan. He regained his dropped sword. Both of my companions stooped over with hands on their knees breathing hard. The vampires surrounded us smiling. They were fresh for a new fight as we were exhausted from fighting ourselves. Defeat clouded my comrade's eyes.

"Stand up straight!" I ordered them. "Fear and despair is what those bastards prey on."

I walked to them and we formed the defensive triangle facing outward. I felt as tired as my friends, but they were totally demoralized as well. Years of training had not taught them to be prepared for this illusion. After almost killing their best friends, I guessed they were hesitant to strike out in offense.

Critter and Bryan stood upright. I reassured them, "Stand tall, men! Keep your eyes open. When the fog comes, open your eyes. All they have are tricks and illusions."

Again, the vampires slowly began to circle us like a pack of wolves searching for the weakest member to attack.

"Eric," Richard pleaded with his smug ass smile, "You may join us. It is not too late."

"Leave these losers and be immortal," another one said.

I didn't answer. I stared forward, eyes resolute to kill any of them who stepped within slashing distance.

I said out loud, "Stand firm men! Call out your names out to each other and keep your eyes open. We can kill these freaks."

I could sense my companions' desire to fight returning and was amazed that I had assumed command over these two who I had greatly feared and admired.

I heard her in my head again, "You should have run. More of us are coming. Joining us is your only way out. Your friends are already dead. You know this. Give up this one battle. You must think of the overall war. You and I can defeat the other vampires later."

The fog started to drift into my field of vision. I realized that I was seeing what Critter and Bryan saw. It was the same feeling I had in the grand throne room where I fell through a blood warm mist. My eyes were closed.

I popped my eyes open as I screamed, "Bryan! Critter! Open your eyes! Answer me!"

"Bryan here! The fog was coming and vanished. Keep the swords ready and eyes open," he said.

"Critter here. Thanks man. We'll beat these creeps."

Richard lifted his sword as the vamps continued their slow circling.

Richard said, "Last chance to walk, Eric. You understand our power better than some already in the brotherhood. Join us."

I heard her in my mind. "Take his offer, Eric, or run, but save yourself."

"All you freaks can go to hell!" I raised my sword up from a defensive position to a striking position above my right shoulder.

"Fool," said Richard. He raised his face to the sky and let loose a horrible shriek. Had I not been holding a sword, I would have been tempted to place my hands over my ears. The other vamps including Abigail joined in. She shot me an apologetic glance and pressed her lips together after finishing the shriek.

I heard the returned sheiks of other vampires who were probably within a half mile of us. They sounded like hellhounds on a trail scented of blood. It sounded like a hundred or more as their horrible ululations echoed through the mountains.

"We need to kill these damn creeps and get the hell out of Dodge before the whole horde of them gets here," said Critter.

"We do not mass in hordes like zombies. Vampires con-gregate in groups called covens," Richard said arrogantly of-fended.

"Screw off, bloodsucker," Bryan hissed.

Both Critter and Bryan backed up into me. From my pe-ripheral vision, I saw Bryan make a small Sign of the Cross from his forehead to chest. I could feel and smell their fear as well as my own. I knew this was turning the vampires crazy for our blood. I could sense them feeding on our terror. I sensed the vampires giving a signal to each other.

Then they physically attacked. They slammed into us with their blades flailing. Bryan, Critter, and I continually called out to each other, for both support and to be sure we didn't ac-cidentally kill each other or fall into the deadly fog of illusion.

Abigail circled in front of me and we crossed swords. I looked her full in the face in the space between our blades.

As she stared at me, she downloaded information in my mind, "We have a circle of power around you. I know you can sense it. If I break it and let you guys run, they will know I have betrayed them. However, if someone else breaks, they won't suspect me. I will take out Lucius. Lucius will be the weak link. When that occurs, you must grab your friends and run through him."

I nodded and looked at Lucius who stood beside her swing-ing at Bryan and me. He was a young vampire probably about twenty. I had slashed him with my sword just last night and it looked like he had fully recovered already.

"Don't look at Lucius like that. He will figure us out," she told me telepathically. The sincerity in her eyes was genuine.

I verbally called out to Bryan and Critter as I listened to her. "Open your eyes Bryan, Critter!"

Bryan answered. Critter didn't.

"Critter." Bryan and I yelled. I could see fog forming. I could see it confined in the circle made by the vampires.

"Critter!" I screamed desperately.

"Yeah yeah," he called back. "These bastards almost had me again," he gasped.

He sounded hopeless. We needed to get out of this mess immediately.

"Hang in there!" I encouraged my comrades.

"Hang in for what?" asked Critter. "I can't see them or fight them."

"Swing at Lucius," Abigail's voice said in my mind.

I swung and immediately realized my mistake in trusting her. I left my belly open for her to slide her blade into me.

But she didn't.

When Lucius' sword blocked my stroke, Abigail's blade quickly and furtively flicked backward and sliced open Lucius' belly instead. He fell to the ground screaming. She shrieked in horror and screamed his name. She attacked me with a few well acted blows of her sword that I barely blocked and then she knelt to care for Lucius.

I stood there staring stupid. Their circle of power was broken. The fog cleared. Bryan and Critter stood straight, lifting their heads and steadying their breaths.

Abigail looked up, glaring at me, "Run, you fools!" The impulse of her telepathic message shook me.

All the vampires shrieked as if they felt Lucius' pain.

I couldn't move.

"Run!" her voice echoed in my head.

I heard the shrieks of the approaching horde of vampires. They were close. The distance measured in mere meters.

I grabbed Critter by the shoulder and pushed him past Abigail. "You're point! Lead!"

Critter started to run.

I grabbed Bryan's shoulder. He started to swing at me and then held back. "Follow Critter. I'll cover the rear!"

"You got it," he said. He still looked in a daze. He hurtled Lucius and crashed into the woods behind Critter.

I looked down at Abigail's exposed neck as she knelt before me. I had a clear opportunity to behead her as she bent over Lucius. I had the same impulse and surge of power that I felt when I punched Bryan at the beginning of this crazy day.

Abigail craned her neck and looked at me. She saw the intent in my eyes and she looked terrified.

"Thanks," I thought at her as I held back my blade and hurdled over her in a great panther-like stride. I could feel her eyes on my back.

We ran. I could hear that the new horde met with Abigail's group as they released their shrieks to the night. They were now in pursuit of us.

Critter stopped and Bryan and I bumped into him. His eyes were dead. I smacked him hard across the face. Clarity came back with a bit of rage.

"Do I need to lead?" I demanded.

He shook his head seemingly as a combination of negating my request and clearing his mind from the mental web that the vampires were spinning.

A cloud covered the moon, plunging the forest into darkness.

Bryan gave him a vicious shove. To an outsider it would have looked like a hateful gesture. However, it was something that Critter needed. He stumbled forward and almost hit the ground before righting himself. He took off running through the dense, trailless woods. Countless branches seemed to purposely grab or smack at us from our own haste. Despite the energy drain of the battle, Critter kept us at a sprint, as could here the howling furies on our heels.

Then I could hear dozens of them in front of us.

"They smell my blood," Critter ranted as he wiped the blood from his throat where Bryan had stabbed him. He stopped leading as we realized that we were surrounded. The mob that we were escaping was a few hundred meters behind. Another group lay about that far ahead.

I heard Abigail in my mind, "Take the lead, hold the sword that I gave you and walk through any group of vampires who confront you. They are faileds and not very bright, but they are deadly. However, they won't attack you with the sword. Trust me."

"Follow me closely," I rasped to my companions as I nudged past Critter. They simply nodded and acquiesced to my command. I jogged with Bryan and Critter on my heels. Ahead I heard the growling and mad grumbling machinations of creatures who devolved beyond humanity.

I slowed to a walk as I saw a group of hunched over, malformed vampires, whose sinister visages were lit up by bloodlust and the pale moonlight. Gone was the intelligence that Abigail, Richard and the others wore on their face and lit their eyes. Only an insane hunger ravaged their faces. Their teeth and fangs were bared. Faces mauled by the fruitless resistance from fingernails and teeth of struggling victims. Most growled or grunted inarticulately. Some muttered curses and profane and blasphemous rages. Some shrieked.

These freaks out numbered us. There were at least thirty in this failed experiment into vampirism. They were armed with machetes, clubs, and other weapons. A few seemed too stupid to carry even the crudest of weapons, but the blood madness in their eyes scared me the most.

Critter and Bryan sheathed their swords and drew their firearms with shaky hands. Their nerves were pulled taut as drum skins. Firearms were weapons of last resort because it drew all manner of monstrosities who feasted on death that resulted from gunfire, but they saw this situation as that dire.

"Hold your fire." I whispered in a harsh command. "This sword will let us walk through. Stay close to me."

They obeyed without a word.

We approached and were within arm's reach of the group when I told my comrades, "Keep your heads up! You own these wild mountains."

The group of filthy monstrosity stared at us as the tip of my blade touched the first one. I stared deep into his blood mad eyes. He smelled of death. He looked down slightly and stepped aside. I kept walking but motioned with the sword for the vampires to move. They grumbled, but complied, parting, and making a path for us, eyes never leaving us.

Bryan and Critter followed close. I dared not look back, but I could feel the electric impulse of the tension in their minds and in their tight grip on their firearms.

All the vampires parted as we walked into the heart of the mob. They were now silent, studying us with their lustful eyes as we were surrounded. Drool dripped from their bared fangs, lips and chins. I felt them ready to pounce at any moment, but it was silent other than the crunch of leaves and heavy breathing. They continued to grudgingly move aside to let us pass.

I forced myself to exhale as I passed the last one, a short squat, hunched over thing, with cancerous growths all over its deformed face, which was streaked with fingernail gouges. It growled suddenly, but was otherwise motionless. The vampires who we just passed slowly filled in the gaps from our wake.

I turned to look back the way we came and point in that direction as I said, "Look that way. You will get all the blood that you desire." I said out loud.

They ignored my command until I shot it through their heads telepathically like an electric impulse like Abigail had suggested..

I continued to walk with my companions and when I was fifteen yards away, I said, "Let's run. Critter, lead."

As Critter took point, I heard the mind ravaging howls and shrieks of vampires far behind. The group we had just passed looked in that direction and returned the cacophonous screams to their hideous kindred, but did not pursue us until they united. I then heard a hideous united scream as they chased us like bloodhounds. Then they all screeched in horrid replies.

"Run," I said.

| 17 |

Even after we could no longer hear their shrieks and footfalls, we still ran hard. Critter constantly looked back at Bryan and me. I didn't know if it was to make sure we hadn't fallen behind or to be sure that he hadn't lost his mind.

We then jogged and quick walked along a trail that headed downhill. We kept this pace up through the dark for another hour or two. Time seemed to lose meaning. Rather than days, minutes, or even seconds, my life was measured in footsteps. We had lives to save back at the camp.

We finally came to a seep where a steady trickle of water flowed from a crack in a rock. Critter looked back at Bryan.

Bryan stopped. Then we all stopped and listened. I heard nothing. Critter nodded to Bryan that it was clear.

Bryan said, "You guys get some water. I'll stand guard."

Critter and I fell to our knees almost in worship before the cold spring. Despite the winter weather, the freezing cold water was a taste of heaven. We had escaped with barely our clothes and weapons. A canteen would have been nice, but

God, when he created the Appalachian Mountains, was very generous with the clean fresh water that flowed naturally from its green and rocky bounty.

Critter and I took turns drinking. The freezy headaches were my prompt to let Critter have a turn to drink. We went back and forth a few times and then Critter stood up, looked to Bryan, and said, "Quench that thirst, brother."

"Thanks," said Bryan as the two men slapped each other on the shoulders.

Bryan knelt on the opposite side of the spring and drank fully from the water that poured into his hands.

"Thank you," Bryan said.

Confused, I was about to ask why he thanked me, but I saw him looking up to the heavens. I stood up and walked back to the trail to stand watch with Critter.

Suddenly on edge, I heard distinctive footsteps in the leaves. It sounded like a large person stalking us. Of course I was immediately on guard for vampires.

"Relax," said Critter. "It's OK."

I looked ahead, expecting to see a human.

Instead, I saw a bear amble into view.

"I never thought I would be relieved to see a bear on a trail rather than a person," I said.

"Those ain't people," Critter said and then spat, aiming off of the trail.

The bear looked at us for a moment and then indifferently walked the other way.

Having consumed his fill of water, Bryan joined in a circle. We sat down. Actually, joined doesn't describe it accurately. Critter, Bryan, and I pretty much collapsed with exhaustion. After the battle and then the run, we needed to recharge and it seemed that our pursuers had given up the chase at least thirty minutes ago.

"What the hell happened back there," Bryan whispered.

Critter, Bryan, and I recounted what we saw and felt. It was a very similar experience between the three of us, but had we not experienced it together, such a tale would have sounded like mad ravings.

Bryan finally said, "Man, I see why we may be the first to have survived an encounter with the vampires. They had us literally at each other's throats."

Critter's hand went to the wound on his neck. It was just a bit deeper than a nick but wasn't anything dangerous, deadly, or debilitating.

"Sorry, bro," said Bryan.

"No problem. I almost did the same to you," said Critter. I'm just glad it's a knife wound from a brother rather than a bite from them.

"Is this what you've been dealing with since last night? You know, the mind games?" Bryan asked.

I nodded.

"Hey, man," Bryan said. "I'm sorry I doubted you. They literally got in my head."

Critter laughed and said, "I thought human women were the masters of mind games. Bro, they ain't got nothing on your girlfriend."

We laughed as quietly as we could, and I said, "She sure as hell isn't my girlfriend."

I sat cross legged and found myself pushing the leaves aside in the circle formed by my crossed legs.

"Abigail is evil in human form," Critter said.

I kept quiet, still mulling what had happened.

"No, she's not." Bryan replied to Critter. I looked up with surprise as he stared straight into my eyes and said, "I don't know what was going on, but we're only here because she saved us."

"What are you talking about?" asked Critter.

I looked curiously at him and he said, "Yeah, I saw her slice that vampire next to her. She sabotaged her own kind to give us a break."

"No kidding?" Critter exclaimed.

"I'm not quite sure what her game is, but the only reason why we're alive now is because of her," I said this as I absent-mindedly dug an inch into the dirt feeling the small rootlets clinging to the soil. The soil was loose, black forest loam.

Bryan sighed and hesitated before saying, "I saw like a fence made of—I feel silly saying this-- magic clouds that disappeared when she sliced him. It was really weird. It looked so real.. Once she sliced him, it broke the spell and he collapsed. It looked like some cheesy special effect for a moment before it vanished. Like one of those movies you saw as a kid and it gave you nightmares for weeks, but then you see it as an adult and it looks so phony and corny. But I saw her look at you, Eric, to get you to run."

That was the longest rambling speech I had ever heard from him. Usually he was brief, prompt, to the point. He was trying to come to grips with something that shook his perception of what was to the core.

I kept digging and felt a round stone. I began to absent-mindedly excavate it.

Bryan finished by saying, "We owe her."

I asked, "Do you think I should try to contact her? You know, through my mind? Or if she contacts me, should I talk or ignore her. She may be a friend, or she may just be playing us for something horrible?"

Bryan took a deep breath in and sighed, "We should talk to Adam about this. Also we should talk more after we're home and rested. I'm so exhausted, it hurts just to think."

"I hear you," I said as I dug up the stone, I studied it. It was rounded and about the size of a hen's egg.

As I looked it over, Critter asked, "Could I have that?"

"Sure," I said as I handed it over.

He studied it in the moonlight and then pocketed it in his jacket as if it passed his inspection.

I could sense that the three of us were getting restless. What had been hot trickles of sweat on my skin now felt as cold as the spring fed rivulet that we had just drunk from.

Critter spoke for all of us, "It's time to go. I hope we get back in time to save Peter."

As we stood, Bryan stretched and said, "You figure it's two or three hours?"

Critter nodded. "I'm hoping we get back just before sun up. I don't like going to bed as the sky turns light."

"I have to take a pee first," said Bryan.

The water from the cold spring was making its way through us.

"Also get one last drink and that should hold us until we're home," Bryan suggested.

I started to walk further into the brush to pee, when Critter, ever the utilitarian, said, "You may as well pee in that place you dug out. It's a pretty good cat hole."

He was correct.

***

We continued on our journey through that long night. I may have been too tired to feel anymore tired if that makes sense, but the run after that wasn't that bad. For one thing, I knew I was running to a nice bed. We weren't running from the vampires anymore or even worse running to their killing fields to rescue Josh. The run also was mostly downhill on a National Forest trail that still benefited from its grooming before the zombie apocalypse.

Occasionally though, Critter would take us off of a trail and cut through rough country. He said that these were combinations of short cuts and to throw off any potential pursuers.

We were on a trail as we crested a ridge line that was sandwiched between two much higher ridgelines. Critter raised his hands to the back of his head, to "expand his lungs," as he put it. His jog slowed to a walk. I knew this meant he was taking a quick break.

As we circled up, I realized that the moon was now hidden behind a cloud. However, I was able to see even better. It was then that I noticed the sun was starting to rise behind us. It wasn't yet manifesting as a redline on the horizon but rather just a faint glow that had nothing but promise.

"Catch your breath. The village is just below us. We should be there in fifteen," Critter said.

I resisted bending over and placing my hands on my knees for support. Instead, I kept myself upright and leaned against a tree. I knew that they respected strength and frowned on weakness. It wasn't a macho thing, but rather it was the one weak link that busted an iron chain. We shared a nod and a smile.

"You're holding up well," Bryan said.

I shook my head no. They looked like they were strong, unaffected by the run and ready to take on a zombie horde. I felt like a hummingbird could knock me over.

"No matter how tired you are, hold your head up high when we enter the village. Don't ever let them see you sweat," Critter advised. "Let's go."

I nodded and realized I had no energy to speak a reply.

Critter took a long step as if to start the run but stopped and looked up in a tree. The first rays of light lit up the branches above. I watched him take the rock that I had dug up earlier from his pocket and place it in a pouch that was attached to two strings. He swung it around on his right side and sent the stone flying up the tree. The rock connected with a squirrel. Both the animal and the rock plummeted to our feet. It was a sling similar to the one David had used to kill Goliath. I was impressed since that was the first time that I had seen it in action. Critter told me later that hitting the squirrel was a 1 in 20 shot for him.

Critter instantly stomped on the dazed squirrel's head to fully dispatch it. He picked it up by the tail to show me, "Breakfast," he announced and then said, "Thanks for the renewable ammo." He pocketed the rock that he had just used.

"Let's go. Bryan, do you want to lead us back?"

Bryan nodded to Critter and he answered by turning his back to us and starting the final leg of the run home.

After a half mile, I heard running water and prayed it was the village's creek. Bryan slowed to a walk and raised his hand for Critter and me to stop and then we slowly entered the village.

Scott looked up and saw us.

"What took you so long? Visited an undead house of ill repute?" Scott greeted us with a typical off color joke of his, but the humor was completely absent from his face and voice. He was too tired, maybe too worried, to even force a laugh at his own joke.

Critter just shook his head solemnly in reply. Then he stopped and looked down at Tomas. He nodded and then pointed his chin at the unconscious man. "How is he?"

"We stayed up all night, talking," Scott said. "Heck, I won't lie. We drank a bit of mead, a little too much. I gots a bit of a headache."

Bryan shrugged it off and said, "This was definitely the time and place for sharing mead."

Scott looked in the air. His lips moved in a spasmed emotional frown, but he kept his composure otherwise, and said, "He made his peace with his maker." Scott looked at me and added, "I think you done burnt the poor guy for nothing," Scott added in reference to my burning Tomas' zombie bite yesterday.

"Sorry," I said weakly.

Scott patted my shoulder and replied, "Don't sweat it buddy. No one has survived a bite that I personally knowed. When it's your time, it's your time. Nothing you or anyone can do about it. No sense sweating it."

We startled as Tomas groaned like he was having a nightmare. He pushed against his bonds and screamed when he couldn't move.

Scott yelled back, "Crap! Scoot back!" he warned us as he raised his sword above his head. "He turned! Tomas turned into a zombie!"

Tomas looked around angrily. As the sword plummeted down towards his head, clarity came to his eyes.

"Stop!" Tomas yelled in a clear, human voice untouched by the grave.

Scott's eyes widened, but momentum was on the side of the sword. Scott tried to stop and redirect the blade as Tomas moved the little that he could against the ropes. The sword nicked his ear and sliced a fissure in his shoulder and upper arm, but it was an easily survivable wound. Scott fell on the ground and apologized profusely. "Man you looked angry. I thought you were a zombie. You said to kill you before-- I mean, you looked crazed."

I noticed that Scott didn't butcher the English language when his heart was full of emotion. I guessed that Bryan was correct that it was part of his goofy act.

Tomas grumpily complained, "You try getting woken up with a hangover from yarrow mead to find that you are tied up and some dumbass redneck is trying to slice you with a katana!"

"Sorry, brother," said Scott.

Tomas continued, "And then the guy who burned off your injury is there too."

I saved him with that burn, but I was too tired to say so.

"You wanna prove that you're sorry ass is really sorry?" Tomas demanded.

"Of course," Scott replied to Tomas.

"Then untie me, ya nitwit!"

Scott looked for permission from Bryan who placed the back of his hand on Tomas' forehead. Bryan said, "He looks fine to me. I don't even see a sign of fever, but I want Adam and Shelly to look him over as soon as he is unbound."

Critter said, "But Bry, he's fine. No one has survived this long with a bite."

"I know. I'm too exhausted to show it, but I am dancing with joy inside, however..." Bryan pinched the bridge of his nose, "protocol," he finally said.

Tomas glared at me, "What the hell are you staring at all gaped mouthed? My arm hurts like hell where you burned me."

"I—"

"Be cool, Tom. He saved your dumb ass," said Critter.

Tomas moved his head back and forth as he considered, frowned and said, "Thanks, Eric."

I just nodded. Having entered the relative safety of the village I could feel things shutting down inside. I just wanted sleep.

"Let's get the antibiotics to Shelley for Peter's broken leg, and then we gotta speak to Adam," Critter said.

"Yeah," Bryan finally said and headed towards Adam's tent.

The old man greeted us at the entrance to his tent. Shelley was with him. Critter handed her the antibiotics and asked, "How is he doing with the broken leg?"

"Horrible," she said, but I think we had some hope now. She looked at the package, "oh good, Clindamycin. This is more than enough to help him and Sarah with her tooth infection also."

Adam looked at us and said, "I heard the good news about Tomas. Shelley and I will go check him out."

"No," said Bryan. "Tomas can wait. Let her work with the broken leg."

Adam looked irritated at his second in command's apparent usurpation of his power. "Then what the hell am I supposed to do?"

"We need to talk."

Adam looked Bryan in the face and realized that the second in command had something weighing heavily on his mind.

"Then talk," Adam said. He waved Bryan into his tent, "Come in. I have some fresh brewed coffee. What's so important?"

Bryan turned and waved for me to follow.

"What's the matter, Bryan?" Adam asked as the old man's suspicious eyes rested on me.

"We have a new and much bigger enemy to deal with than we could ever have imagined. We know why no one has survived a vampire attack until recently. Eric actually knows more than I do."

With a cup of coffee, we discussed the vampires, The Specter, and Craig for over an hour. Adam, for all his wisdom, had his mind blown. The only decision we made was that we changed one of the rules. From now on, three people must always stay together when venturing into the woods rather than just two. After a good sleep through the day we would view the video I had from the encounter with the vampires.

Tomas was irate with the delay, but freed later that morning and made a full recovery. Peter, the man with the broken leg had his infection stabilized, but his recovery prevented us from leaving the campsite for a few days.

I finally went to bed shortly after the meeting. That was the first time Abigail talked to me in my sleep. It wasn't a dream though. It was something more real than a dream. She warned me to stay away from her. Under penalty of death, she was ordered to turn me. I knew she could slip in and out of our camp past our sentries, but underneath the terror that I felt, I had to admit to myself that I had feelings for my deadly ally.

| 18 |

Epilogue

A few days later

Back in his temporary headquarters, Tommy kept an eye on his computer monitors. He was dressed in one of his nicer blue business suits. He had scheduled a helicopter to take him back to Washington DC for the New Oscar awards. California was in a quarantine zone and the venue had been changed to a more central location when entertainment became a mix of propaganda, intelligence gathering, and amusement for the masses. Tommy was slated to win an Oscar for his documentary work that resulted from his work specifically with drones. However, tonight he would not just receive an award he would announce the release of his new reality show.

The footage and commentary gathered by Eric would make it more personal. Tommy's stardom was virtually assured. He had a brilliantly heartwarming speech ready to give. He knew it was vapid, but that's what sold. He wasn't proud of it, but he was a realist.

On the wall behind Tommy hung a poster with the title "Mountain Warriors" spread across the top. It was just delivered today. Under the headline and in the foreground of the Appalachian scenery stood Eric, Bryan, Anna, and their kids, along with Shelly and Adam. With them were The Specter, an anonymous hooded vampire, Abigail with her hood slightly down with a sexy smile and a bare shapely thigh photo shopped in, and of course, Tommy. They were all clustered together as if they met there for a production photo op. It was all photo shopped for effect.

Tommy finished adjusting his collar and straightening his tie and then he pressed a button on his desk. The door opened and Don Renton entered the room. The big man had a fresh bandage on the side of his shaved cranium from the punch that Eric delivered with the pistol. Don glared at the poster and gave it the finger. "'Mountain Warriors!'" his voice boomed irritably. He threw the skull faced mask of The Specter on the desk.

"I see you dislike the new design," Tommy said.

"Craigsville would have been a better show than following those hillbillies." Don growled

Tommy sighed. "That idiot Eric is screwing up our plans. I thought he would take the path of least resistance rather than be the resistance. But I think this may work out. In the short term, it will put some of our plans on hold, but I find the characters in that mountain tribe to be more... interesting than those folk in Craigsville. This was a fortunate mishap."

"I don't know," said Don. "You should send me into that tribe and let me kick some ass. Or strafe it with a Blackhawk."

"Don, we will get what we want. This is simply a detour. A detour that may make us filthy rich in the process. You let your ego get in the way of financial gain, my friend. The mountain tribe has a much grittier tale for us to tell. Another detour seems to be coming from one of the vampires, but you saw that coming, eh Don?"

"Speaking of vampires, did Eric--?" Don left the question hanging. He had been in other parts of the Forbidden Zone for the last few days.

"No. Check this out," Tommy said as he clicked a screen. Don squinted his eyes as they watched Critter, Bryan, and Eric stand in a triangle formation facing outward. Bryan and Critter, swung wildly at the space in front of them as the vampires circled far beyond their sword reach. Eric stared intensely at Abigail. Tommy pointed at Abigail and Lucian.

"Look," Tommy said as he motioned to the two young vampires. "None of the humans are near them and suddenly when the drone's camera leaves them, the young male vampire falls as if from a sword stroke."

They watched as the footage pulled away and focused on Bryan and Critter. When the footage went back, it showed Abigail kneeling at Lucian's side.

Tommy said, "Either, he sliced himself, the vampire on the other side did it, or our rebel vampiress is again the little culprit."

Don nodded, "I'm starting to agree with you. We should kill her. If she's guilty of even a fraction of what we suspect of her--"

"No, no, no," Tommy said. "I'm beginning to like her. She creates a stirring story."

"The department of science grows tired of her lack of co-operation."

"What of her psionic abilities?" Tommy asked.

"What use are they if she uses them to sabotage our program? The department is close to issuing an order to have me terminate her. They want to dissect her brain to see why she has her abilities and why she rebels."

"Try to buy her some time," Tommy pleaded.

"You obsess too much over your silly show."

Tommy sighed, "It's intelligence gathering. Speaking of which, I have to get to Washington. I can hear my chopper approaching."

"Break an arm," Don said.

Tommy stopped walking and looked confused.

""Showbiz," Don said.

Tommy laughed as he figured it out and said, "Oh you mean, break a leg. Breaking arms and busting heads is your job. Speaking of which, you got your noodle whacked pretty good."

"Oh, I'll get back at Eric for this," Don said as the two men left Tommy's office. "I'm heading back in as we speak."

Tommy tightened his lips as he watched his former right hand man turned loose cannon leave his office.

To be continued.

EXCERPT: BOOK 3

The most action packed yet. Coming out in late October 2021, just in time for Halloween!

"...but he was Alexander the Great. Not Eric the Journalist." I said.

Bryan shrugged off my worry and replied, "He was only the 'Great' because he had a chance to prove it. You are not called Eric the Great by others simply because you were never given a chance to lead a cavalry charge at the age of sixteen. You're no different from Alexander. Here is your chance! I'm relying on you with this mission."

I felt my blood run cold as I figured out where he was going...

LATER THAT DAY

...I stood on a slight rise in the valley and raised my sword.

"Alright, men! Let's go!" I spoke deep and loudly. I then screamed with all my soul, "Charge!" I pointed my blade dramatically towards the 200 zombiebot formation guarding the fortress where my friends were held prisoner. The zombiebots outnumbered us, but we were motivated.

I heard the men around me scream as they followed my running charge. They were right behind me. I saw a man fall to my left as I heard the crack of the sniper's rifle. I screamed louder and charged harder. I shot through the open gate and felt the surge of an adrenalin rush as I led my men. I smashed into the formation of the zombiebots, slashing with my sword and felt myself taken over by a berserker rage. I slashed through six or seven zombies ducking their swinging blades. I slashed through three or four more zombiebots and mounted the top of the front porch.

I realized I was exhausted and breathing hard, but gung ho and motivated to fight on. I didn't expect to make it to the steps so quickly. It was an adrenalized three hundred yard sprint with fighting. It took a toll and I was foolish to burn myself out so quickly, but there wasn't time to rest. I cleared the rest of the zombies off the porch as they fought each other to taste my blade.

Having accomplished that goal, I turned to face my men and swore bitterly. They were one hundred yards behind battling the first ranks of the zombies. I had been the only one to smash my way through. I was now surrounded by hundreds of zombies. I looked for my right flank that was to launch a surprise attack from the side and saw that they were just now making a weak charge far beyond the walls of the compound. I quickly looked away as the zombies charged me. Surrounded by the horde and no one ally at my back, I was screwed.

FOR READERS

Do you want more? Can't wait until the next book? Would you like to read short stories by the author? Check out rjburle.com. Sign up for the e-newsletter and get access to short stories. You can even request that R.J. write a short story to get background information on characters who don't get enough attention or main characters who you would like to understand better.

Also, if you have any questions on anything* in the book, particularly in outdoor survival, fighting techniques, etc. and would like to see the author demonstrate it, contact him through the website and he will demonstrate it on his YouTube channel. The author turned 50 years old in 2021 and looks forward to a challenge.

*Anything does not include illegal activities, something life threatening, live slayings of monsters who don't exist in real life, etc. :)

ABOUT THE AUTHOR

R.J. Burle's interests are as far flung as hunting with home-made archery equipment to spending a few years as a volunteer firefighter, from trapping and SCUBA diving to even earning a doctorate in Chiropractic. He is a student and teacher of martial arts--studying many forms throughout his life. He studied screenwriting at UCLA, and he incorporates that fast paced style of writing into his novels. The former Marine is married with four kids and credits living a colorful life with having a deeper well from which to draw inspiration. His first novel, *Outcast*, was published in October 2020 and is the first in the Mountain Warrior series. Visit him online at rjburle.com.